JAMIE'S JOURNEY

JAMIE'S JOURNEY

TONY MEDLEY SR

Contents

First Printing, 2025
Printed in the United States of America.

Paperback ISBN: 979-8-9934305-5-3
Ebook ISBN: 979-8-9934305-6-0

Publisher: Medley Publishing Group

Introduction

Life is not a collection of random moments—it is a journey marked by valleys of struggle, peaks of victory, and winding roads of discovery. For those who believe, this journey is never traveled alone. It is guided by the eternal voice of God. His Word—the divine conversation spoken before time began—echoes through every generation, inviting us to walk in His truth, embrace His promises, and live in His abundant grace.

Jamie's Journey is a fictional novel woven with biblical principles, eternal truths, and the raw realities of life. At its center stands Jamie, an ordinary young man with extraordinary potential. Like so many of us, he wrestles with questions of identity, purpose, and faith. Though his path is marked by challenges that threaten to pull him away from God's spoken truth, Jamie's story reveals the transformational power of believing God's Word above every competing voice.

Rooted in the teachings of the author's earlier work Wrapped in the Conversation, this novel brings to life the truth that God's Word—His Logos, His divine conversation—surrounds, defines, and sustains us. These foundational realities are woven into Jamie's lived experiences, becoming the canvas upon which God paints His promises with bold, hopeful, and sometimes painful strokes.

As you follow Jamie's path, you will watch him stumble and rise, question and believe, wander and return. You will witness the power of pisteuo—faith that entrusts every part of life to Christ. You will see him learn to meno—abide, continue, and remain in God's Word. And you will experience his awakening through ginosko—the knowing, perceiving, and declaring of truth that sets him free. Jamie's struggles are relatable, his questions honest, and his victories inspiring.

Yet this book is more than a story—it is an invitation. Each chapter not only pulls you into Jamie's world but invites you to reflect on your own. Whose words shape your identity? What conversations have you been living under? Are you burdened by shame or covered in glory? Your answers will shape how you walk out the abundant life Jesus promised.

In these pages, Scripture's timeless message is expressed through story. The goal is not merely to entertain, but to awaken faith, stir hope, and strengthen your walk with God. As Jamie's journey unfolds, may your own journey find renewed courage, deeper conviction, and a greater trust in the One who has spoken life over you.

Turn the page. Step into Jamie's story. Allow his journey to illuminate your own. And may you discover, as Jamie does, that when you cling to the conversation God has spoken over your life, you cannot lose—for in Christ, you are already victorious.

Preface

Every book begins with a burden, and Jamie's Journey is no exception. The burden on my heart was clear: to show, through story, how God's Word is not a distant echo from an ancient time, but a living conversation that still surrounds and shapes our lives today.

In my years of ministry and teaching, I have seen how many believers know the promises of God in their heads but struggle to carry those promises into their everyday lives. We quote Scripture, we nod in agreement to sermons, but too often, when trials come, we forget the conversation that heaven is having about us. This disconnect has left too many people walking in defeat when they were called to victory.

That is why Jamie's story had to be told. Though fictional, his journey is deeply real. He represents every believer who has wrestled with doubt, stumbled under the weight of temptation, and struggled to reconcile what God has said with what life seems to show. Jamie's questions are our questions. His battles mirror our own. And his victories point us back to the truth that we can never lose when we remain in God's Word.

This novel is not meant to replace Scripture but to bring its truths into a narrative that we can see and feel. The Greek words—pisteuo (to believe), meno (to continue), logos (the Word), ginosko (to know), and so many others—are not mere theological terms but anchors for living. They are woven throughout this story as reminders that God's promises are not abstract ideas; they are daily realities waiting to be embraced.

My prayer is that as you read, you will not only follow Jamie's transformation but also reflect on your own journey. Ask yourself: What conversation am I living under? Do I walk in the truth of what God has declared, or in the lies of the enemy? Am I living free, or am I still bound by fear, shame, or doubt?

The preface is often the place where authors thank those who helped bring a project to life, and I would be remiss not to do so. To every reader of my earlier work Wrapped in the Conversation, thank you. Your feedback, prayers, and testimonies inspired me to expand those truths into story. To my family and ministry partners who continually remind me of God's faithfulness—this book is as much yours as it is mine.

Above all, I give thanks to God, the Author of life, who first spoke the words, "Let there be light," and has been speaking ever since. It is His conversation that sustains us, redeems us, and crowns us with victory in Christ Jesus.

As you turn these pages, may Jamie's journey awaken something fresh in your spirit. May you rediscover the joy of believing, the strength of abiding, and the power of walking in the truth that makes us free. And may this book not simply be read but lived.

— Dr. Tony E. Medley Sr.

Foreword

Stories have always been one of God's most powerful tools. From the parables Jesus told to the testimonies of saints throughout history, narratives capture truth in ways that sermons alone sometimes cannot. They allow us to see ourselves in the struggles of another, to feel the weight of their trials, and to rejoice in their victories.

Jamie's Journey is one such story. Though fictional, it is deeply real because it reflects the universal struggles of the human heart—the longing to know God, the battle against shame, the temptation to listen to false voices, and the ultimate triumph that comes when we embrace the Word God has spoken over us.

Dr. Tony E. Medley Sr. has given us more than a novel; he has given us a testimony in story form. Rooted in biblical truth and enriched by insights from Wrapped in the

Conversation, this book demonstrates what it means to live daily under the covering of God's Word. Each chapter unfolds like a mirror, inviting the reader to examine their own life. Are we listening to the lies of the enemy or to the voice of God? Are we clothed in shame or wrapped in glory? Do we remain in His Word when the storm rages, or do we step out into the noise of other conversations?

What makes this work so compelling is its balance. It is both inspirational and practical, both imaginative and deeply scriptural. Jamie is not presented as a flawless hero but as an authentic human being—uncertain, flawed, yet pursued and transformed by the relentless love of God.

Through his journey, we see our own potential to be more than conquerors through Christ.

By the time you reach the final chapter, you will not simply have read a story; you will have encountered a call. A call to believe, to abide, to know, to remain, to present yourself under the Conversation of God. And like Jamie, you may find your life reshaped in ways you never expected.

As you begin this journey, I encourage you to do more than just follow Jamie's story. Let it push you to consider your own. Ask yourself: What conversation defines me?

Whose words am I living under? If you let it, this book will do more than entertain—it will challenge, convict, and ultimately point you closer to Christ, the true Word made flesh.

May Jamie's Journey awaken fresh faith in you, stir new courage within you, and remind you that God's Conversation over your life is still active, still true, and still victorious.

1

Believed on Him

The sound of rain tapped steadily against Jamie's apartment window, a rhythm that seemed to echo the unsettled beat of his heart. He leaned against the sill, watching the blurred city lights shimmer beneath the storm. It had been one of those weeks—the kind where everything felt fragile, like a house of cards one wrong move away from collapse.

Work deadlines piled high, his friendships felt distant, and the loneliness of his quiet apartment pressed in like a heavy fog. He rubbed his temples, wishing he could silence the constant stream of doubts and fears that haunted him.

He turned toward the small wooden desk in the corner of the room. On it lay his Bible, edges worn and the leather cover softened by years of half-hearted reading. Tonight, though, he felt drawn to it differently. Not as a routine, not out of guilt, but almost as if it were calling to him.

Jamie pulled out the chair, sat down, and opened the Scriptures. His eyes wandered over verses until one word caught him. It was familiar, but somehow new: believe.

He had seen the word countless times before, but tonight, curiosity nudged him to look deeper. He reached for a study guide his grandmother had given him years ago.

7

Slowly, he traced the Greek translation. The word leapt off the page: Pisteuo.

He whispered it aloud, letting the syllables linger in the quiet: "Pisteuo."

The study note explained: to have faith in or upon; to entrust for one's well-being.

Jamie blinked. This wasn't about a shallow nod of agreement or mentally assenting to God's existence. No—it was more demanding, more intimate. It called for trust. Not partial trust, not a cautious half-measure, but the kind of trust where a man lays the full weight of his being into God's hands.

Entrust. The word struck him deep.

He pushed back from the desk and sank into the couch, staring at the ceiling. Entrusting his well-being sounded beautiful—and terrifying. His life had been one long lesson in disappointment. His father had promised to be there for Little League games, but rarely showed up. His first serious relationship ended with words that cut like glass: "You're not enough." Even friends had proven unreliable, fading away when his struggles became too heavy for them to carry.

Trust was not something Jamie gave easily anymore. He closed his eyes, and memories washed over him.

Nights lying awake as a boy, listening for the sound of his dad's car pulling into the driveway. The way his heart had lifted each time he thought maybe—just maybe—his father would keep his word. The crushing silence that followed when the car never came.

Entrust? He clenched his fists. How could he entrust himself fully to anyone? Even to God?

And yet, another voice inside—soft, insistent—whispered: What if this time is different? What if the One asking for your trust will never betray it?

Jamie exhaled slowly. He turned back to the Bible and read again: believed on Him.

The preposition "on" mattered. It wasn't merely believing in the existence of God, as one believes in gravity or history. It was believing upon Him—placing the full weight of his life, his identity, his future, his well-being, on Christ. It was leaning not on himself, but on the One who had already carried the cross and conquered death.

He reached for his journal, its pages half-filled with random notes and unfinished prayers. Tonight, the words came easier, though his hand trembled as he wrote.

Lord, I want to believe on You. Not just with my head, but with my heart. I've been let down too many times to trust easily, but if Your Word is true, then teach me. Show me what it means to entrust my whole life into Your hands.

The words blurred as tears welled in his eyes. Jamie wasn't used to crying. He had built his life around keeping emotions in check, always being the strong one, always pretending everything was fine. But here, alone with God, the walls cracked.

He set the pen down and bowed his head. The silence in the room felt alive, almost expectant.

"God," he whispered, his voice hoarse, "I don't know how to do this. But I want to. I want to believe on You. I want to entrust myself—my whole self—to You."

For a moment, nothing happened. Then, slowly, a peace unlike anything he had ever known settled over him. It wasn't loud or dramatic. It was quiet, steady, like a river flowing deep beneath the surface. His breathing slowed. The tightness in his chest eased. It was as if unseen arms had wrapped around him, steadying him, assuring him that he was finally safe.

Jamie leaned back, eyes closed. For the first time in years, he felt the faint flicker of hope.

The next morning, Jamie woke earlier than usual. The rain had cleared, leaving the city washed and glistening in the sunrise. He brewed a pot of coffee and sat once more with his Bible. The word Pisteuo was still open on the page.

He thought of his grandmother, the one who had first introduced him to Scripture. She had passed away a few years earlier, but her voice still lingered in his memory. She used to say, "Jamie, don't just believe in God like you believe the sun exists. Believe on Him like you'd lean on a rock when you're weary. He won't let you fall."

At the time, he had brushed off her words. But now, they returned with power. She had been talking about this very moment, this deeper faith that required surrender.

As he sipped his coffee, Jamie realized the decision he made last night wasn't the end—it was the beginning. Entrusting himself to God wasn't a one-time act; it was a daily posture. Each day, he would face the choice: to lean on his own understanding, or to believe upon Christ.

The thought both steadied him and scared him. Because he knew that life had a way of testing belief.

Later that day, at work, Jamie sat at his desk surrounded by the usual noise of ringing phones and clicking keyboards. He worked in logistics, coordinating shipments and solving problems that seemed to multiply faster than he could resolve them. Normally, the stress pressed hard on his shoulders. But today, he found himself pausing mid-task, whispering a simple prayer: Lord, I entrust this to You.

It felt awkward at first, almost childlike. But with each whispered prayer, the burden grew lighter.

During lunch, he shared a table with his coworker, Marcus, who noticed the difference.

"You seem... calmer today," Marcus said, raising an eyebrow. "What's up? You finally win the lottery or something?"

Jamie chuckled. "Not exactly. Just... trying to live differently."

Marcus smirked. "What, like meditation or yoga?"

Jamie hesitated. Part of him wanted to keep it private, but another part sensed this was an opportunity. "No. More like trusting God. Really trusting Him."

Marcus laughed. "Man, that's risky business. God doesn't exactly cut checks or fix shipping errors."

Jamie smiled faintly. "Maybe not directly. But... I'm starting to believe He's involved. That He cares. That I can entrust myself to Him."

Marcus shook his head. "Good luck with that, man. I've learned the only one you can trust is yourself."

Jamie nodded slowly, but inside, a conviction stirred. That's exactly what he had believed his whole life—that only he could protect himself, that trusting others was weakness. But last night had changed something. For the first time, he wasn't leaning on himself. He was leaning on God.

That evening, Jamie returned home exhausted but strangely uplifted. He sat once more at his desk, opened his Bible, and whispered again, "Pisteuo."

He thought of the word like a foundation stone, something he could build his life upon. It wasn't fragile like human promises. It was steady, unshakable.

As the night stretched on, Jamie sensed that this was just the beginning. Life would test his decision. There would be days when faith felt impossible, when fear screamed louder than hope. But tonight, he had chosen. He had placed the full weight of his life into the hands of God.

And though he didn't know what the road ahead would hold, Jamie knew this much: he would not walk it alone.

2

Believer in Christ

The morning light streamed through the thin blinds of Jamie's apartment, golden rays breaking apart the shadows of the night. For the first time in a long time, Jamie woke up with a sense of anticipation rather than dread. He stretched, rubbed his eyes, and let the quiet of the early hour sink into him.

Something was changing.

He couldn't fully explain it yet, but since the night he had prayed to entrust himself to God, life looked different.

The problems were still there—work deadlines, financial pressures, the dull ache of loneliness—but they didn't feel as heavy. There was a thread of hope running beneath everything, pulling him forward.

He shuffled to the kitchen, brewed a pot of coffee, and sat at the small wooden table where his Bible still lay open.

As he poured a steaming cup, his eyes fell again on the words he had underlined the night before:

"If you continue in My word, then are you My disciples indeed. And you shall know the truth, and the truth shall make you free." (John 8:31–32)

He traced the verse with his finger. If you continue...

The word "continue" gripped him. It wasn't about a single moment of faith, as powerful as that was. It was about a daily, deliberate choice to walk in the Word. To keep leaning in, to keep believing, even when life pulled him in the opposite direction.

Jamie leaned back in his chair and whispered aloud, "I am a believer in Jesus. And I know He will deliver what is best for me."

The words hung in the air. Speaking them out loud gave them weight, as though he were planting a flag in the ground of his own soul.

A Lesson at Work

Later that morning, Jamie walked into the office, briefcase in hand. The familiar noise greeted him—the phones ringing, coworkers murmuring, the clatter of keyboards. Normally, the tension of this place drained him before the day even began. But today, he carried something different.

At mid-morning, a crisis erupted. A major shipment had gone missing in transit, and the client was furious. Jamie's boss stormed into the office, barking orders. Stress shot through the room like electricity.

Jamie felt the old panic rise in his chest. His mind raced with worst-case scenarios. But then he paused. *If I continue in His Word...* The verse flashed through his memory. He bowed his head slightly, unseen by those around him, and whispered, *Lord, I trust You. I'm a believer in You, and I know You'll deliver what's best.*

He picked up the phone and began making calls. To his surprise, doors opened faster than usual. A supplier admitted they had misrouted the shipment and promised to expedite corrections at no extra cost. By the end of the day, the issue was not only resolved but the client received a discount for the inconvenience.

Jamie leaned back in his chair, exhaling a long breath. It wasn't luck—it was God's hand. The situation that could have spiraled into disaster had turned around for good.

As he gathered his things to leave, Marcus, his coworker, gave him a curious look. "Man, I don't know how you do it. Everyone else was losing their minds today, and you were... calm."

Jamie hesitated. The easy answer would be to shrug it off. But something within him pushed for honesty. "I've been learning to trust Jesus with everything. He's teaching me not to panic, but to believe that He'll deliver what's best for me."

Marcus chuckled, shaking his head. "Faith, huh? Sounds good in theory. But the world doesn't exactly run on Bible verses."

Jamie smiled faintly. "Maybe not. But I'm learning that it runs on more than what I see. And God has a way of showing up when you least expect it."

Marcus didn't respond, but the flicker of curiosity in his eyes told Jamie that a seed had been planted.

The Weight of the Word

That night, back in his apartment, Jamie couldn't shake the verse from John 8. He opened his journal and wrote:

"Being a believer isn't about one prayer. It's about continuing. Continuing in His Word when I'm tired. Continuing when I'm afraid. Continuing when I don't understand. Lord, help me not just start this journey but to keep walking it every day."

He thought about his grandmother again. She used to say, "Jamie, your faith isn't measured by how loud you shout or how high you jump on Sunday. It's measured by how you walk on Monday morning. Continue in His Word, and He'll continue to hold you."

Tears stung his eyes. He wished she were still here to see him now, finally beginning to live out what she had prayed for.

Temptation to Quit

A few days later, Jamie faced another test. He received a phone call from his younger sister, Rachel. Their mother's health was declining again, and the doctors were recommending expensive treatments insurance wouldn't fully cover.

Jamie felt his stomach sink. Money was already tight, and he had been saving just enough to keep himself afloat.

Fear whispered: *See, this is why you can't trust anyone but yourself. You'll have to figure it out. God won't show up this time.*

For a moment, the old Jamie—the self-reliant, anxious one—rose to the surface. He sat on his bed, head in his hands, tempted to believe the lie. But then, slowly, he remembered: I am a believer in Jesus. And I know He will deliver what is best for me.

He said it aloud, over and over, until the words felt stronger than the fear. Then he opened his Bible, searching for promises. His eyes landed on Matthew 6:33: "Seek first the kingdom of God and His righteousness, and all these things will be added unto you."

Jamie closed his eyes. "Lord, I don't know how You'll do it. But I trust You. Deliver what's best—for Mom, for Rachel, for me."

That weekend, an unexpected breakthrough came. An old family friend, who had once owed Jamie's mother a debt of gratitude, offered to cover a significant portion of the medical costs. The relief was overwhelming.

Jamie sat in his car after hearing the news, whispering through tears, "Thank You, Lord. You really do know what's best."

Living as a Believer

Over the weeks that followed, Jamie began to build new rhythms. Each morning, he read a chapter of Scripture before work. Each night, he journaled prayers and reflections. When problems rose, he reminded himself: *Continue in His Word.*

It wasn't always easy. Some days he felt weary, some days doubts still crept in, but there was a growing consistency in his faith. He was no longer just a man who had once believed—he was a man who was learning to live as a believer.

At church one Sunday, Jamie found himself singing with a sincerity he hadn't known before. The words of the hymn weren't just lyrics—they were declarations of his new identity. He wasn't a man defined by his failures or fears anymore. He was a believer in Christ.

And as he left the service, a quiet assurance filled him. The road ahead would bring challenges, yes. But he was not walking it alone. He had a Savior who would deliver what was best for him—as long as he continued in His Word.

Foreshadowing

That evening, Jamie sat by his window again, watching the city lights flicker against the night sky. His Bible rested on his lap, his journal open beside him.

He wrote: "I am a believer in Christ. This is who I am now. And I will continue in His Word—not just for today, but for tomorrow, and for every day after. Lord, strengthen me to keep believing, even when storms come."

As he laid the pen down, he sensed it deep within his spirit: storms would indeed come. His faith would be tested, perhaps in ways he could not yet imagine. But tonight, he was ready. Tonight, he knew who he was.

He was Jamie, a believer in Christ. And that made all the difference.

3

Continue

The city was alive with its usual rhythm—horns blaring in traffic, footsteps echoing on sidewalks, voices rising and fading like waves on a restless ocean. Yet inside his apartment, Jamie felt none of that motion. He sat still at his desk, Bible open, journal nearby, heart heavy.

The past few weeks had been a whirlwind. First the crisis at work, then the ongoing stress of his mother's health, and now an unexpected financial strain. It felt like the very moment he had declared himself a believer in Christ, the weight of life had doubled.

He tapped his pen nervously against the edge of the journal, staring at the page but not writing a single word. His eyes drifted to the margin notes in his study Bible. A single word caught his attention: Meno.

The definition was simple yet profound: To stay or abide in a given place, state, relation, or expectancy.

Jamie read it again, slower this time, letting the meaning sink in. To stay. To abide. To continue.

He leaned back, exhaling. He had always been quick to move on when things got hard. Friendships that grew messy, jobs that became stressful, even church experiences that demanded too much of him—he had often found reasons to slip away. Staying was not his strong suit.

But now, God was calling him not just to believe once, not just to declare faith in a moment of inspiration, but to continue. To remain. To abide in Christ even when nothing seemed to change.

Staying When It's Hard

The following Monday, work hit him with another storm. A client pulled out of a contract unexpectedly, leaving Jamie's team scrambling to adjust shipments and costs.

His boss was furious, and the atmosphere in the office was tense.

By lunch, Jamie's chest felt tight. Anxiety pressed in, whispering, *This isn't working. You trusted God before, but look at this. You're on your own.*

He pushed away from his desk and went outside. The city air was cool against his face. He walked down the block until he found a small bench under a tree, away from the noise. Sitting down, he buried his face in his hands.

"God," he whispered, "I don't know how much more I can take."

For a moment, silence pressed in. Then a verse surfaced in his memory, one his grandmother had quoted often: "Abide in Me, and I in you."

Abide. Stay. Continue.

Jamie lifted his head, staring at the leaves above him. He realized that faith wasn't about escaping the storm—it was about staying rooted through it.

He prayed softly, "Lord, help me to remain. Even here. Even now."

Something inside steadied. The problems didn't vanish, but the panic loosened its grip. He rose from the bench, straightened his shoulders, and walked back to the office with a quiet resolve.

The Power of Abiding

That evening, Jamie sat at his kitchen table with his Bible still open to John 15. His eyes scanned the words slowly:

"Abide in Me, and I in you. As the branch cannot bear fruit of itself unless it abides in the vine, neither can you, unless you abide in Me. I am the vine, you are the branches. He who abides in Me, and I in him, bears much fruit; for without Me you can do nothing."

He underlined the verse, whispering, "Without You, I can do nothing. But if I stay... if I continue... fruit will come."

Jamie pulled out his journal and wrote:

"Faith isn't just about believing once. It's about remaining —day after day, even when I don't see results. Abiding isn't passive; it's active trust. It means I choose to stay in Christ, stay in His Word, stay in expectancy. Lord, help me not just to start this journey but to continue in it."

He closed the journal, exhaling. For the first time, he saw that abiding wasn't weakness—it was strength. The branch didn't bear fruit by striving, but by staying connected.

A Conversation with Rachel

A few days later, Jamie stopped by Rachel's apartment to drop off groceries. Their mother's treatments were ongoing, and Rachel had been carrying much of the daily burden of care.

As Jamie unpacked items onto the counter, Rachel glanced at him curiously. "You've been different lately," she said.

Jamie paused, lifting an eyebrow. "Different how?"

"You're not as restless. Even with everything going on, you seem... steady."

Jamie leaned against the counter, thinking. "I've been learning what it means to continue. To abide in Christ. To stay rooted even when things don't make sense. It's not easy, but it's changing me."

Rachel frowned. "But isn't that just... waiting around? Doesn't it feel like you're doing nothing?"

Jamie shook his head slowly. "It's not doing nothing—it's expectancy. Like a branch connected to a vine. The branch isn't lazy just because it's not producing fruit every second. It's abiding. It's staying connected to the source. And the fruit comes in time."

Rachel looked thoughtful but didn't reply. Jamie noticed, though, that her eyes softened, as if the idea touched something in her.

Expectancy in the Waiting

In the weeks that followed, Jamie began to build small rhythms of expectancy. Each morning, before work, he prayed not just for solutions but for strength to remain. On his commute, he whispered Scriptures to himself. At night, he wrote down prayers—not as desperate cries but as declarations of trust.

One entry read: "Lord, I don't see the breakthrough yet, but I expect it. You promised that if I abide in You, fruit will come. I will stay. I will continue."

Even in moments when discouragement pressed hard, expectancy anchored him. He began to notice small signs of God's faithfulness—a kind word from a stranger, an unexpected provision, moments of peace in the middle of chaos.

They weren't dramatic miracles, but they were reminders that God was present.

The Test of Remaining

One Thursday evening, Jamie received a call from Rachel. Their mother's condition had worsened, and the doctors weren't optimistic. Fear gripped him as he sat listening.

After hanging up, Jamie sank onto his couch, his heart heavy. Tears welled in his eyes as he whispered, "God, why is this happening? I thought if I trusted You, things would get better. Why does it feel like it's getting worse?"

For a long while, he sat in silence, the weight of grief pressing down. Everything in him wanted to run—to escape the pain, to stop hoping so he wouldn't be disappointed.

Then he remembered the word: Meno. To stay. To abide. To continue.

Through tears, Jamie prayed, "I don't understand. But I'll stay. I'll trust. I'll continue in You, Lord. Even here."

Peace didn't erase the pain, but it wrapped around him like a blanket. In that moment, he knew the power of abiding wasn't that it avoided sorrow—it was that it held him steady through it.

Fruit in Due Season

Weeks later, a small breakthrough came. Though their mother's health didn't fully improve, she experienced unexpected strength and joy in her final days. She spoke words of blessing to Jamie and Rachel, reminding them of the faith she had carried all her life.

Jamie wept as he realized: the fruit of abiding wasn't always the outcome he expected, but the transformation it brought within him. He was stronger, steadier, rooted in Christ in a way he had never been before.

One night, he sat by the window, city lights glowing beneath the stars. He opened his journal and wrote:

"Meno—continue. Abide. Stay. Lord, I will remain in You. In every season, in every state, in every relation, in every expectancy. My life is not about running from hardship but about staying rooted in You. And in time, fruit will come."

He closed the journal, a quiet resolve filling him.

Jamie knew storms would still come. Life would still bring challenges. But he also knew this: he was no longer a man who gave up easily. He was learning to abide.

And that single choice—to continue—would carry him through the journey ahead.

4

The Word

The morning was quiet, almost unnaturally so. Jamie sat at his kitchen table, coffee steaming in his mug, Bible open before him. The city outside was its usual blur of noise, but inside, there was stillness.

He had been reading through the Gospel of John, and this morning he stopped at the opening verses:

"In the beginning was the Word, and the Word was with God, and the Word was God." (John 1:1)

He read it again, slower this time, whispering the words aloud. Something about them felt different, as though the page itself was alive.

Word. Logos.

Jamie reached for his study guide, flipping until he found the explanation. The Greek word was Logos—Divine Expression, God's conversation, His thought, His intention revealed. It wasn't just letters or sentences. It was the very voice of God, eternal and unchanging, yet present in every moment of his life.

Jamie set the guide down, his heart stirring. So the Bible isn't just a book—it's God's conversation with me.

Discovering the Divine Conversation

As he sat there, Jamie thought back on the many times he had skimmed over Scripture without really listening. He had treated it like a textbook or a rulebook, not realizing it was alive with God's own thoughts.

But now, something inside him shifted. The Word was not only divine—it was personal. It wasn't written to "people in general"; it was written for him, to him, over him.

He whispered, "Lord, what are You saying to me?"

His eyes dropped again to the verse: "The Word was God."

Jamie's breath caught. If the Word was God, then every time he opened the Bible, he wasn't just reading—he was meeting the living Christ.

He felt tears sting his eyes. All the loneliness, the times he had felt unseen, the nights he had cried silently—suddenly, he realized he had never been alone. God had been speaking all along.

A Renewed Mind

Later that day at work, Jamie noticed something strange. In the middle of a meeting, when tempers flared over logistics, a verse popped into his mind: "Be quick to hear, slow to speak, slow to anger." (James 1:19)

Normally, Jamie would have jumped into the argument, eager to defend his point. But the Word shifted his response. He stayed quiet, listening carefully. By the end of the meeting, his calm approach helped de-escalate the tension.

As he walked back to his desk, he realized something: the Word wasn't just changing how he prayed—it was reshaping how he thought, how he acted.

"Be transformed by the renewing of your mind." The verse from Romans 12 came alive. The Word was rewiring him from the inside out.

A Battle in the Mind

That night, though, the battle came. Jamie sat alone, staring at the ceiling, doubts flooding his thoughts. *You're not strong enough. You'll fail like you always have. This faith won't last.*

The voices felt relentless. For years, these lies had defined him, shaping his choices and limiting his courage.

But this time, another voice rose within him—the Word.

"You are a new creation in Christ."

"Greater is He that is in you than he that is in the world."

"I will never leave you nor forsake you."

Jamie sat up, speaking the verses aloud into the darkness. His voice shook, but the truth pushed back the lies.

"This is God's conversation over me," he said firmly. "Not my failures. Not my fears. His Word."

Peace slowly settled over him. The battle wasn't over, but he had found his weapon.

A Conversation with Marcus

The next day at work, Marcus noticed Jamie scribbling something in his notebook during lunch.

"What are you always writing in there?" Marcus asked, half curious, half mocking.

Jamie smiled, tapping the cover. "Scripture. God's Word. It's how I remind myself of what's true."

Marcus raised an eyebrow. "So you're telling me some old book is shaping your life?"

Jamie nodded. "It's not just a book. It's a conversation. God speaks through it. And it's changing the way I think."

Marcus laughed, shaking his head. "Sounds crazy, man. But... you do seem different. More... grounded, I guess."

Jamie's smile widened. "That's because the Word is alive. It's not just words on a page—it's Him. And when I let His Word get into me, it changes everything."

Marcus didn't answer, but Jamie noticed he didn't laugh as hard this time.

Living Logos

In the weeks that followed, Jamie built a rhythm. Each morning, he read not just to check off a box, but to listen. Each verse became part of a larger conversation. He wrote them in his journal, spoke them aloud, carried them with him into meetings, into phone calls, into quiet nights when fear returned.

He realized that abiding wasn't only about staying—it was about staying in the Word. Staying in the Logos, letting the divine expression of God's heart saturate his own.

Some days it felt effortless, other days it was a battle. But slowly, his inner life began to change. The lies grew quieter. The truth grew louder. His mind was being renewed, his thoughts aligned with heaven's conversation.

One night, Jamie sat by his window, journal open, city lights glowing below. He wrote:

"The Word is God's conversation with me. Every time I read, I'm not just seeing ink—I'm hearing His thoughts, His heart, His voice. Lord, help me to live in Your Word, not just read it. Let Your Logos reshape me, renew me, and guide me. I will continue in Your Word, because Your Word is life."

He closed the journal, peace washing over him. The journey wasn't easy, but he was no longer alone. He was wrapped in the Word—God's living, breathing Logos.

And that Word would carry him forward.

5

The Disciple

The church basement smelled faintly of coffee and fresh paint. Folding chairs lined the room in a circle, and a few people were already seated, Bibles open on their laps.

Jamie hesitated at the doorway, clutching his own Bible against his chest.

It had been months since he first whispered that prayer of belief, months of learning to abide in Christ's Word, months of wrestling with fears and doubts. But now he sensed God calling him deeper. Not just to believe, not just to abide, but to learn.

He stepped inside, quietly taking a chair near the back. The group leader, a kind older man named Pastor Dan, greeted him warmly. "Glad you're here, Jamie. Tonight we're talking about discipleship."

Jamie's heart quickened. He had been reading about discipleship in his own study, the word Mathetes catching his attention. It meant student, learner, follower. But not just any learner—an active learner. Someone who didn't just listen but practiced, lived out, embodied the teachings of the Master.

Pastor Dan began, "To be a disciple isn't just to agree with Jesus. It's to follow Him, to learn from Him daily, to shape your life around His words."

Jamie scribbled notes furiously in his journal. He had always thought of Christianity as a set of beliefs to affirm. But this was different. This was apprenticeship.

The Call to Learn

That week, Jamie carried the word Mathetes with him everywhere. At work, when Marcus joked about his faith, Jamie reminded himself: *I am a disciple, a student. Every conversation is a classroom. Every challenge is a lesson.*

When his sister Rachel vented about the stress of caring for their mother, Jamie resisted the urge to fix everything. Instead, he listened—really listened—and remembered Jesus' words: "Love one another as I have loved you."

At night, as he journaled, Jamie wrote:

"Being a disciple means I don't just hear Jesus' words—I live them. I don't just know about Him—I learn from Him. Every day, I'm in His classroom."

The realization both excited and intimidated him. It was easier to keep faith abstract, but discipleship demanded action.

A Lesson in Forgiveness

One Friday evening, Jamie faced one of his hardest lessons yet. He ran into an old friend, Mark, who had betrayed his trust years earlier. Seeing him brought old bitterness rushing back.

They exchanged awkward greetings, and as Jamie walked away, anger churned inside him. *I can't forgive him. Not after what he did.*

But then the words of Jesus echoed: "Forgive, and you will be forgiven."

Jamie clenched his fists. Forgiveness wasn't just a nice idea—it was a command. And if he was truly a disciple, a student of Christ, then this was a test.

That night, he knelt by his bed, tears stinging his eyes. "Lord, I don't want to forgive him. But if I'm Your disciple, teach me. Help me learn this lesson."

It didn't happen overnight. But slowly, through prayer, Jamie felt the weight of bitterness lift. He wasn't excusing what Mark had done, but he was releasing him into God's hands.

And in that act, Jamie realized: discipleship wasn't theory. It was transformation.

Training the Heart

Weeks turned into months, and Jamie began to see every area of life as discipleship. His time in the Word became more focused. He wasn't just reading for inspiration; he was studying, asking, *What is the lesson here? How do I live this out?*

When tempted to cut corners at work, he remembered, *A disciple walks in integrity.*

When tempted to doubt, he remembered, *A disciple stands on the Word.*

When tempted to give up, he whispered, *A disciple continues, abides, stays.*

He began to see that discipleship wasn't a course with an end date—it was a lifelong apprenticeship. Every day was a new assignment, every struggle a new lesson, every blessing a new reminder of the Teacher's presence.

A Conversation with Marcus

One afternoon, Marcus leaned on Jamie's cubicle, shaking his head. "You really take this faith thing seriously, don't you?"

Jamie smiled. "It's not just faith. It's discipleship. I'm a student of Jesus. Every day He's teaching me how to live."

Marcus raised an eyebrow. "So what's He teaching you now?"

Jamie paused, then chuckled softly. "Right now? Forgiveness. Patience. And probably humility."

Marcus smirked. "Sounds like a tough teacher."

Jamie shook his head. "No. He's the best teacher. Because He doesn't just give lessons—He walks through them with me."

For once, Marcus didn't joke. He just nodded thoughtfully and walked away.

The Apprentice of Christ

That night, Jamie sat by his window, journal open. The city lights shimmered like stars scattered across the ground.

He wrote:

"A disciple is more than a believer. A disciple is an active learner. Lord, I don't want to just know about You—I want to know You. Teach me. Shape me. Make me more like You. Every day, in every moment, let me be Your student."

As he closed the journal, Jamie felt a deep sense of calling. His journey wasn't just about believing, abiding, or hearing the Word. It was about living as a disciple—actively learning from Christ, every day, for the rest of his life.

And that realization changed everything.

6

Know the Truth

The words had echoed in Jamie's heart all week: "You shall know the truth, and the truth shall make you free."

He had heard the verse countless times growing up, but it always felt like a distant promise, reserved for preachers or theologians. Now, after months of believing, abiding, and walking as a disciple, the verse came alive.

He dug deeper into the Greek and discovered the word: Ginosko.

To know—not just intellectually, but experientially. To allow. To be aware. To perceive. To be resolved. To be able to declare.

Jamie closed his Bible and whispered, "Lord, I don't want to just know about the truth. I want to know it. I want to live free."

A Subtle Lie

That week, Jamie faced an unexpected challenge. During a routine meeting at work, his supervisor hinted that he should adjust some numbers in a report to make their division look more profitable. "It's not a big deal," the man said with a smile. "Everyone does it. Just a little creative reporting."

Jamie froze. The old version of him might have gone along, rationalizing it as survival. But something deep inside resisted. The Word stirred within him: "You shall know the truth, and the truth shall make you free."

He realized this was more than a workplace dilemma. It was a battle between truth and deception, between freedom and bondage.

Jamie spoke carefully. "I'm sorry, but I can't do that. It wouldn't be honest."

His supervisor's smile faded. "Think about it, Jamie. You've got a good future here. Don't throw it away over something small."

Jamie's pulse quickened, fear gnawing at him. But he walked away knowing he had made his choice.

The Weight of Awareness

That night, Jamie sat in his apartment, replaying the conversation. Fear whispered: *You're going to lose your job. You'll regret this.*

But another voice—firmer, truer—rose within him: *You are walking in truth. And the truth makes you free.*

Jamie opened his journal and wrote:

"To know truth is to perceive it, to recognize it even when others call it small or harmless. Truth is not negotiable.
Lord, make me aware of Your truth in every situation, even the subtle ones. Let me be resolved."

As he wrote, he felt chains breaking inside him. Lies about survival, fear of man, the pressure to conform—they no longer had the same hold. Freedom wasn't just about external circumstances. It was about being free on the inside.

A Conversation with Rachel

A few days later, Jamie visited Rachel. She was stressed, overwhelmed by their mother's care and her own job.

"I don't know how to do this anymore," she confessed, her voice breaking. "It feels like I'm drowning."

Jamie sat beside her, listening. Then he gently took her hand. "Rachel, can I share something I've been learning?"

She nodded, eyes wet.

"Jesus said the truth makes us free. And the truth is... you're not carrying this alone. God hasn't abandoned you. He's here, and He's strong enough for both of us. The truth is, you are loved. You are seen. You are held."

Rachel wept openly, leaning into his shoulder. For the first time, Jamie realized that knowing the truth wasn't just for himself. It was something he could declare to others, setting them free too.

The Power to Declare

That Sunday, during worship at church, Jamie felt a stirring in his spirit. When the pastor asked if anyone had a testimony, Jamie surprised himself by standing.

With trembling hands, he took the microphone. "I've been learning what it means to know the truth. Not just in my head, but in my heart. And I've realized that truth isn't just a concept—it's a Person. Jesus said He is the Truth. And when you know Him, when you perceive Him, when you resolve to stand with Him, you find freedom you didn't think was possible."

The congregation erupted in amens, but Jamie's eyes filled with tears. For the first time, he wasn't just reading the verse—he was living it. He knew the truth, and he was free.

Living Free

In the days that followed, Jamie carried a new awareness. Every time fear whispered, every time lies pressed in, he countered with truth.

When he worried about the future, he declared: "The Lord is my Shepherd; I shall not want."

When shame tried to rise, he declared: "There is no condemnation for those who are in Christ Jesus."

When doubt clouded his vision, he declared: "I can do all things through Christ who strengthens me."

Knowing truth wasn't passive. It was active. It was declaring what God had said until it became more real than the lies.

And slowly, Jamie began to walk lighter. The chains that had bound him for years—fear, shame, insecurity—began to fall away.

Freedom in the Word

One night, Jamie sat by his window again, journal open, city lights glowing below. He wrote:

"Know (Ginosko)—to allow, to be aware, to perceive, to be resolved, to declare.

Lord, I choose to know Your truth. Not just to read it, but to live it, to declare it, to walk in it. Thank You that Your truth makes me free."

He closed the journal, exhaling deeply. The journey wasn't over—there would be more battles, more lies to confront, more lessons to learn. But now, he carried a weapon stronger than fear: the truth.

And in that truth, he was free.

7

The Eternal Truth

Jamie leaned back in the worn pew of the small church, the soft hum of the organ fading as Pastor Dan opened his Bible. The room was quiet except for the sound of pages turning.

"Tonight," Pastor Dan said, "we're looking at the book of Revelation. And I want us to pay attention to how Jesus describes Himself—Alpha and Omega, the First and the Last."

Jamie's eyes dropped to Revelation 1:8: "I am Alpha and Omega, the beginning and the ending, saith the Lord, which is, and which was, and which is to come, the Almighty."

He circled the verse in his Bible, his heart quickening. Alpha—the beginning. Omega—the end. The First and the Last.

Later, in his study guide, Jamie saw the Greek word: Aletheia. Truth. Derived from Alpha, the first. Not just a statement of fact but the eternal reality that Jesus is the Truth, the origin and the completion of all things.

Jamie whispered, "So truth isn't just what's correct—it's Who was first. It's Jesus Himself."

Knowing the First

That night, Jamie couldn't sleep. He sat by the window, journal open, staring at the city lights. For years, he had built his life on shifting ground—opinions, circumstances, his own fragile strength. But now, he realized truth wasn't relative. It was absolute, eternal, rooted in the First.

He wrote:

"Aletheia—truth that begins in Alpha. To know the truth is to know the First, the One who was before all things.
And when I know Him, I am free."

Tears filled his eyes as he whispered, "Lord, You are the First. You've always been there, even when I thought I was alone. Teach me to anchor my life in Your eternal truth."

A Test of Foundation

The next week, Jamie's foundation was tested. His supervisor called him into the office. "Jamie, about last week's report..."
Jamie's stomach tightened.
"I've decided to let you go," the supervisor said bluntly. "You're a good worker, but we need team players who don't question instructions."

The words hit like a punch to the gut. Jamie gathered his things in silence, anger and fear swirling inside. By the time he reached his apartment, his faith felt shaken.

Sitting at his desk, he buried his face in his hands. *This is what I get for standing on truth? For refusing to compromise?*

But then his Bible fell open to Revelation 22:13: "I am Alpha and Omega, the beginning and the end, the first and the last."

Jamie's tears fell onto the page. He realized—jobs could come and go, people's opinions could shift, but the Truth remained. Jesus was still Alpha, still Omega. He was still the First and the Last. And that truth was unshakable.

Jamie whispered, "Lord, You are the First. If I know You, I'm free. Even now."

Peace slowly replaced fear. His circumstances hadn't changed, but his foundation had.

A Conversation with Rachel

When Jamie told Rachel about losing his job, she looked at him with wide eyes. "What are you going to do?"

Jamie smiled faintly, surprising himself. "I don't know yet. But I know this—Jesus is the First and the Last. He's my Alpha and Omega. My life doesn't begin or end with this job. It begins and ends with Him."

Rachel studied him for a long moment. "You really believe that, don't you?"

Jamie nodded. "I know it. Not just in my head—in my spirit. And that truth makes me free."

The Eternal Perspective

Over the next few weeks, Jamie experienced God's faithfulness in unexpected ways. A friend connected him with a new job opportunity that aligned more with his gifts. Provision came through in ways he hadn't expected.

But more importantly, Jamie carried a new perspective. He no longer measured truth by circumstances. Truth was eternal. Truth was Alpha. Truth was Christ Himself.

One evening, he sat again at his window, journal open. He wrote:

"Aletheia—truth rooted in Alpha. The First and the Last. Lord, help me to live every day anchored in You, not in shifting circumstances. You are the eternal Truth. And knowing You is freedom."

He closed the journal, peace washing over him. He was no longer afraid of losing what could be taken away. He had found the One who could never be taken.

And that Truth was enough.

8

Free

The air was heavy with summer heat as Jamie walked through the park near his apartment. Children's laughter echoed from the playground, and the scent of grilled food drifted from a family picnic nearby. Yet despite the life around him, Jamie's heart was troubled.

He had been reading about freedom in Christ, but the weight of his past clung stubbornly. Mistakes, regrets, and failures rose like ghosts to haunt him. He whispered to himself, *If I'm supposed to be free, why do I still feel chained?*

That night, he sat at his desk, Bible open. His eyes fell on Galatians 5:1: "Stand fast therefore in the liberty wherewith Christ hath made us free, and be not entangled again with the yoke of bondage."

He traced the words with his finger. *Made free.* The Greek word: **Eleutheroo**.

He opened his study notes: *To liberate. To exempt from moral, ceremonial, or mortal liability. To deliver. To make free.*

Jamie leaned back, whispering, "To liberate... to deliver... to make free."

A thought struck him — freedom wasn't just the absence of chains. It was the active deliverance of a Savior who broke them.

The Weight of Shame

That week, Jamie's struggle with shame came to a head. He met with an old acquaintance from college, and their conversation turned to the reckless choices Jamie had made back then — the drinking, the failed relationships, the compromises.

"You've really changed," the man said with a smirk. "But I still remember the old Jamie. Hard to see you as some 'man of faith' now."

Jamie forced a smile, but the words cut deep. By the time he got home, shame wrapped around him like chains.

He sat in the dark, whispering, *Maybe I haven't really changed. Maybe I'll always be that guy deep down.*

But then the Word rose within him: "If the Son therefore shall make you free, ye shall be free indeed." (John 8:36)

Jamie spoke it aloud, shaky but firm: "I am free indeed. Jesus has liberated me. I am not who I was."

It felt awkward, almost unnatural, but as he repeated it, something shifted inside. He realized that freedom wasn't about forgetting the past — it was about being delivered from its power.

The Chains Break

The following Sunday, Jamie went to church with a heavy heart. During worship, the pastor began to speak about freedom.

"Freedom," the pastor said, "isn't just a legal statement. It's a lived reality. In Christ, you are exempt from condemnation. You are delivered from the penalty of sin. You are liberated from bondage. You are free."

Jamie felt the words pierce his soul. Tears streamed down his face. He lifted his hands and whispered, "Lord, I receive it. I am free."

In that moment, it was as if invisible chains fell from him. The shame, the guilt, the fear that had bound him loosened. He realized freedom wasn't something he had to earn. It was something Jesus had already given.

A Conversation with Rachel

Later that week, Jamie sat with Rachel, who was weary from caring for their mother.

"I feel trapped," she admitted. "Like no matter what I do, I'm failing."

Jamie took her hand. "Rachel, I've been learning something. Freedom doesn't mean life is easy. It means you're no longer chained by guilt or fear. Jesus liberates us, delivers us, makes us free. And that freedom gives us strength to keep going."

Rachel's eyes filled with tears. "Do you really believe that?"

Jamie nodded. "I don't just believe it. I'm starting to live it."

Living Delivered

Over the next few weeks, Jamie began to practice freedom daily. When fear whispered, he declared liberty. When shame rose, he remembered he was exempt from condemnation. When temptation pulled, he leaned on the truth that he was delivered.

One night, he journaled:

"Eleutheroo — to liberate, to deliver, to make free. Lord, thank You that I am no longer bound to my past. Thank You that I am not defined by failure. Thank You that I am free — truly free — because of You."

He closed the journal, peace filling him. He realized that freedom wasn't a feeling that came and went. It was a reality secured by Christ. And each day, as he walked in it, the chains grew weaker, until they were nothing but shadows of a life already redeemed.

A New Boldness

Jamie noticed the difference everywhere. At work, he walked with new confidence, no longer weighed down by fear of failure. At church, he worshiped freely, no longer hiding in the shadows of guilt. With friends, he spoke openly about his faith, no longer ashamed of who he had been.

For the first time in years, Jamie felt light — truly light.

One evening, as the sun dipped low and painted the sky with hues of gold and crimson, Jamie stood on his balcony and whispered, "I am free."

The words weren't just a declaration. They were a song. A truth. A reality.

He was free.

9

The Well Kept Secret

The church was quiet in the late evening. Candles flickered at the altar, casting long shadows across the sanctuary. Jamie sat alone in a pew, his Bible open to Psalm 91.

"He that dwelleth in the secret place of the most High shall abide under the shadow of the Almighty."

He whispered the verse aloud, tasting the words slowly. *Dwelleth. Secret place. Shadow of the Almighty.*

Something stirred inside him, something deeper than before. He had always read Psalm 91 as a promise of protection — safety from danger, security in storms. But tonight, he felt as though the verse held a hidden key. A well-kept secret, waiting to be unlocked.

He reached for his study notes. The Hebrew word for *dwelleth* caught his attention: **Yashab** — to sit down, to remain, to marry.

Jamie blinked, stunned. *To marry?*

He whispered, "So dwelling in God's presence isn't just about staying close. It's about covenant. About intimacy. About union."

The thought shook him. He had always seen his relationship with God as devotion, obedience, discipleship. But marriage? That was something different. Marriage was permanent. Marriage was exclusive.

Marriage was union.

The Marriage Covenant

Jamie dug deeper, flipping through cross-references. Romans 7:1–6 spoke of being released from the law through death and now belonging to Christ, "married" to Him in newness of life. Deuteronomy 24 outlined laws of marriage and covenant.

Jamie's mind raced. *This is the well-kept secret.* Dwelling with God is not just visiting His presence. It is sitting down, as one sits to marry. It is binding myself to Him in covenant.

He felt the weight of it settle in his heart. This wasn't about rules or rituals. This was about relationship — covenant intimacy with the Almighty.

Jamie closed his eyes and whispered, "Lord, I want to dwell with You. Not just occasionally visit Your presence, but live in covenant with You. I want to sit down — to marry You with my whole life."

A New Kind of Intimacy

Over the next few days, Jamie carried the thought everywhere. At work, on the train, in the quiet of his apartment, he found himself reflecting: *Am I visiting God, or dwelling with Him?*

He realized how often his faith had been episodic. He prayed when in need, worshiped when at church, studied when inspired. But God was calling him deeper — not to moments, but to marriage.

That night, he journaled:

"To dwell (Yashab) is to sit as if to marry. Lord, forgive me for treating our relationship casually. I choose covenant. I choose permanence. I choose You, not just sometimes, but always. Teach me to live as one who has sat down to marry You."

The Shadow of the Almighty

As Jamie pressed into this truth, he began to notice subtle shifts. Anxiety that once gripped him loosened its hold. Fear of the future grew quieter. He sensed God's presence more constantly, not just in prayer but in the ordinary.

One evening, as he sat by his window, he whispered Psalm 91 again: "He that dwelleth in the secret place of the most High shall abide under the shadow of the Almighty."

He imagined himself literally sitting under the vast wings of God, like a bride under her husband's covering. The imagery was powerful. The shadow wasn't distance — it was protection, intimacy, closeness.

Jamie realized that to dwell in the secret place was not only safety — it was union. It was covenant belonging.

A Conversation with Marcus

At lunch, Marcus noticed Jamie's peaceful demeanor. "You've been different again," Marcus said. "What's your secret?"

Jamie smiled. "The secret place."

Marcus raised an eyebrow. "What's that supposed to mean?"

Jamie leaned forward. "It's from Psalm 91. God doesn't just want me to pray sometimes or check in when things go bad. He wants me to dwell — to sit down with Him as if to marry Him. To live in covenant with Him every day. That's the well-kept secret of peace and freedom."

Marcus shook his head, half-amused. "So you're married to God now?"

Jamie chuckled. "In a way, yes. And I've never felt more secure."

Marcus didn't reply, but Jamie saw the curiosity in his eyes. Seeds were being planted.

Covenant Confidence

Weeks passed, and Jamie's life reflected the shift. Challenges still came, but he no longer faced them as a man alone. He faced them as one in covenant with the Almighty.

When fear whispered, he declared: "I dwell in the secret place. I abide under the shadow of the Almighty."

When temptation came, he reminded himself: "I am married to Christ. I belong to Him."

When loneliness rose, he whispered: "I am not alone. I dwell with Him always."

One night, as he journaled, Jamie wrote:

"The well-kept secret is this: to dwell with God is to marry Him. To sit down permanently in covenant union. This is where freedom lives, where peace flows, where protection abides. Lord, I am Yours — forever."

He closed the journal, tears in his eyes. He knew now that his journey wasn't just about learning, obeying, or even being free. It was about union. Covenant. Marriage with the One who loved him first.

And that well-kept secret would carry him deeper than he had ever gone before.

10

Spirit

The late afternoon sun poured through Jamie's apartment window, warming the wooden table where his Bible lay open. His eyes lingered on Psalm 91 once again. It had become his anchor, the well-kept secret of dwelling with God. But this time, one word caught his attention: Spirit.

As he dug deeper into his study notes, the Greek word surfaced: **Pneuma** — the rational soul, the inner disposition, the very breath of God. From *Pneo*, meaning "to breathe."

Jamie whispered it aloud. "Pneuma. The breathed air of God."

He leaned back in his chair, staring at the ceiling. If dwelling with God was like sitting down in covenant, then living by the Spirit was like breathing His very breath.

Breath of Life

Jamie thought back to Genesis, where God formed Adam from the dust of the ground and breathed into his nostrils the breath of life. Man became a living soul because God's breath filled him.

He whispered, "So my spirit lives because of His Spirit. Every breath I take is a reminder that I am sustained by Him."

Jamie closed his eyes, inhaling slowly, exhaling deliberately. For the first time, he practiced breathing with awareness of God's Spirit. Each inhale became a prayer: "Come, Holy Spirit." Each exhale: "I belong to You."

It was simple. Yet profound.

The Mental Disposition

Later that week, Jamie noticed his thoughts drifting toward old patterns of fear and negativity. At work, when a project stalled, his first instinct was to spiral into worry.

But then he remembered: *Pneuma* — the rational soul, the mental disposition.

"Spirit," he whispered under his breath, "reshape my thinking."

As he prayed, a calmness filled him. Ideas surfaced that helped resolve the problem, and his coworkers were surprised at his steady attitude.

Jamie realized the Spirit wasn't just about emotional highs in worship. It was about renewing his mind, reshaping his mental disposition, training him to think like Christ.

Covered in the Secret Place

That Sunday, Pastor Dan preached again from Psalm 91. "The Hebrew word for secret here," he said, "is **Cether** — it means covering, disguise, protection."

Jamie's heart leapt. He scribbled furiously in his journal:

"Spirit and secret are linked. The Spirit is the breath of God, and the secret place is His covering. Together they protect me, guide me, and hide me from the enemy."

He pictured himself hidden under the vast shadow of the Almighty, covered, disguised, safe. Not invisible to the world, but invisible to the schemes of the enemy.

A Conversation with Rachel

That evening, Jamie visited Rachel. She looked exhausted, dark circles under her eyes.

"I feel like I'm under attack from every side," she confessed. "Work, bills, Mom's health... I can't breathe."

Jamie sat beside her, taking her hand. "That's exactly it," he said softly. "Breathe. God's Spirit is His very breath. Let Him fill you."

Rachel looked skeptical, but Jamie led her through the same breathing prayer he had practiced. Inhale: "Come, Holy Spirit." Exhale: "I belong to You."

Tears rolled down her cheeks as she whispered the words. For the first time in weeks, her shoulders relaxed.

Jamie smiled gently. "That's the secret place. The Spirit is our covering, our disguise, our protection. When we breathe Him in, we rest under His shadow."

Spirit in the Battle

A few days later, Jamie faced his own test. Late one night, waves of anxiety gripped him. Thoughts of failure, fear of the future, loneliness — they all pressed in at once.

But this time, instead of fighting in his own strength, he turned to the Spirit. He lay flat on the floor, breathing deeply, whispering, "Holy Spirit, breathe on me."

Slowly, the heaviness lifted. Peace wrapped around him like a blanket. The battle wasn't gone, but he was hidden — covered, disguised, protected in the Spirit's secret place.

Living by the Spirit

In the weeks that followed, Jamie began to see life differently. He realized that every thought, every decision, every breath was shaped by the Spirit.

When negativity tried to dominate, the Spirit renewed his mind.

When fear tried to suffocate, the Spirit breathed life.

When danger loomed, the Spirit became his covering.

One night, as he journaled, he wrote:

"Pneuma — the rational soul, the breathed air of God.

Cether — the secret covering, disguise, protection.

Lord, I will dwell in Your Spirit. Let every thought, every breath, every step be filled with You. Cover me in Your secret place, hide me from the enemy, breathe on me daily."

He closed the journal, inhaled deeply, and exhaled slowly.

For the first time in his journey, Jamie realized that life with God wasn't just about belief, discipleship, or even freedom. It was about being sustained by the Spirit — the very breath of God, the secret covering of His presence.

And with that breath, he knew, he could face anything.

11

Covered

The night was stormy, rain pelting against the windows of Jamie's apartment. He sat at his desk, Bible open to Psalm 91, reading slowly over verse 4:

"He shall cover thee with His feathers, and under His wings shalt thou trust: His truth shall be thy shield and buckler."

He whispered the words. "He shall cover thee…"

The word **cover** caught his attention. He reached for his notes and found the Hebrew term: **Cakak** — pronounced *Sawkak*.

To entwine as a screen.

To fence.

To join together.

Jamie leaned back, stunned. He had always imagined "cover" as a shield, a barrier that blocked danger. But this definition painted a richer picture: entwining, fencing, joining together. God's covering wasn't just defense. It was intimacy.

He whispered, "Lord, You don't just block the storm. You entwine Yourself with me. You join Yourself to me."

The Fence of His Presence

The next day, Jamie walked through the park, reflecting on the word. He passed a wooden fence, its slats joined tightly together. The sight struck him deeply.

"That's what covering means," he thought. "Not just a wall between me and danger, but a joining together — me and Him, woven like wood and nails, entwined like threads of a garment."

He realized God's covering was not distant protection, but near intimacy. To be covered was to be joined.

Exodus 33:22

Later that week, Jamie dug into the cross-reference. Exodus 33:22. Moses on the mountain, desperate to see God's glory. God's response: "And it shall come to pass, while My glory passeth by, that I will put thee in a cleft of the rock, and will cover thee with My hand while I pass by."

Jamie closed his eyes, imagining the scene. The Almighty placing Moses in the cleft, then covering him — **Cakak** — entwining, shielding, holding close.

His eyes filled with tears. "That's what You do for me, Lord. You hide me in Yourself. You cover me with Your hand. You entwine me with Your presence."

A Conversation with Rachel

That evening, Jamie shared the revelation with Rachel.

"Think about it," he said. "God's covering isn't just a shield. It's Him entwining Himself with us, joining Himself to us like a fence woven together."

Rachel looked thoughtful. "So... being covered isn't about running from trouble. It's about being held close, even in it?"

Jamie nodded. "Exactly. Like Moses in the cleft of the rock. God didn't remove the storm of His glory — He placed Moses inside safety, covered him with His own hand. That's what He does for us."

Rachel smiled faintly, the weight of worry softening in her eyes.

Covered in the Storm

A week later, Jamie faced his own storm. He received an unexpected bill in the mail that threatened to wipe out his savings. Panic clawed at him.

But then he remembered: **Cakak** — to entwine, to fence, to join together.

He knelt beside his bed, spreading the bill before God. "Lord, cover me. Entwine Yourself with me. Fence me in with Your presence."

As he prayed, peace washed over him. The storm didn't vanish immediately, but he felt sheltered. Hidden. Covered. He knew God would make a way.

And within days, an unexpected financial provision arrived, enough to cover the need.

Jamie wept with gratitude. "You covered me, Lord. You really did."

Woven Together

Over the next few weeks, Jamie saw covering everywhere. In the way branches interlaced overhead, forming natural shade. In the way threads of fabric joined to create strength. In the way fences were built, piece by piece, stronger together than alone.

He realized God's covering wasn't fragile. It was woven, interlaced, entwined — a bond that could not be broken.

That night, he journaled:

"Cover — Cakak. To entwine, to fence, to join together. Lord, thank You for covering me, not from a distance but up close. Thank You for entwining Yourself with my life, for fencing me in with

Your presence, for joining Yourself to me in covenant.
I am safe. I am covered."

The Strength of the Covering

At church the following Sunday, the choir sang a hymn about being hidden under God's wings. Jamie lifted his hands, tears streaming. For the first time, he fully understood what it meant.

To be covered was not weakness. It was strength. It was the Almighty entwining Himself with him, fencing him in, holding him safe.

Jamie whispered, "I am covered."

And he knew it wasn't just a verse anymore. It was reality.

12

Who Shall Deliver Me?

Jamie sat in his apartment late into the night, Bible open, heart heavy. He had been reading Romans 7, and the words cut him deeply:

"For the good that I would I do not: but the evil which I would not, that I do. ... O wretched man that I am! Who shall deliver me from the body of this death?" (Romans 7:19, 24)

He closed his eyes, whispering, "That's me. Paul just described me."

For weeks, Jamie had felt the tension inside. He wanted to walk in holiness, but temptation tugged at him. He wanted peace, but fear kept creeping in. He wanted to trust fully, but doubt knocked at the door.

He clenched his fists. "Who shall deliver me?"

The Word Deliver

The next day, Jamie dug into the word "deliver." In Greek, it was **Rhoumai** — to rescue, to draw out, to reserve. From the root word **Rheo**, meaning *to flow as a river*.

Jamie blinked at the definition. "To flow as a river..."

He whispered it again, "Deliverance isn't just being snatched away from danger. It's being drawn into a flow — like a river carrying me forward."

The thought shifted everything. He realized he had been treating deliverance as a one-time escape, a sudden snatching away from struggle. But God was showing him that deliverance was also about flow — about movement, about grace carrying him daily.

The Struggle

That week, Jamie's struggle came to a head. At work, Marcus pushed his buttons with crude jokes. On the way home, an old temptation rose to call someone from his past. By evening, he felt drained, caught between desire and conviction.

Slamming his journal shut, Jamie cried, "God, I don't want to keep failing like this! Who will deliver me?"

And then the verse echoed: "Thanks be to God, through Jesus Christ our Lord." (Romans 7:25)

Jamie collapsed to his knees. "Jesus... You are my deliverer. Not just once, but every day. Deliver me now. Let me flow in Your river."

As he prayed, a strange peace washed over him. It wasn't that the struggle disappeared, but he felt carried — like a river lifting him, moving him, enabling him to go forward without sinking

A Conversation with Rachel

Later that week, Jamie shared his discovery with Rachel.

"Romans 7 feels like my life," he admitted. "Wanting to do right, but messing up anyway. Feeling like I'm stuck in this cycle."

Rachel nodded slowly. "I know that feeling too."

"But here's what I learned," Jamie continued. "The word deliver in Greek doesn't just mean rescue. It means to draw out, to flow like a river. Jesus doesn't just snatch us once. He carries us daily, like water flowing around rocks. That's how we get through."

Rachel's eyes filled with tears. "So freedom isn't about never struggling. It's about being carried by Him through the struggle?"

Jamie smiled. "Exactly. The river doesn't stop at obstacles. It flows through them. And Jesus is that river."

Flowing Like a River

In the days that followed, Jamie began to picture his life as a river. When temptation came, he prayed, "Lord, keep me in Your flow." When discouragement rose, he whispered, "Carry me through."

He noticed the difference. The struggles didn't vanish, but they no longer drowned him. He was learning to let grace carry him like water.

One evening, as he sat by the window watching rain fall onto the streets, he whispered, "Deliverance isn't me fighting harder. It's me flowing with You, Jesus. You are the river."

Covered and Carried

One night, Jamie woke from a troubling dream, heart racing. Fear clawed at him, but then Psalm 91 came to mind again: "He shall cover thee..."

And he realized: God's covering wasn't just protection — it was also movement. The same hand that covered Moses in the cleft was the hand that carried him through.

Jamie prayed softly, "Cover me. Carry me. Deliver me. Flow through me like a river."

And peace returned.

Living in the Flow

Over the next few weeks, Jamie leaned into the rhythm of deliverance-as-flow. He stopped condemning himself when struggles arose and instead learned to yield to Jesus as the river.

At church, he shared his testimony: "I used to think deliverance meant I'd never struggle again. But now I know — it means Jesus carries me through the struggle. Like a river, He keeps me flowing. That's how I'm delivered — not because I'm strong, but because He is."

The congregation erupted in amens, and Jamie felt the chains of condemnation break a little more.

The Daily Cry

One night, Jamie journaled:

"Who shall deliver me? Rhoumai — to draw out, to flow like a river.

Jesus, You are my deliverer.

Deliverance isn't about escape, but about flow.

You carry me like water around rocks, through valleys, over obstacles.

You don't just rescue once. You deliver daily.

And I will trust You to keep me in Your river."

He set down his pen, breathing deeply. The war within him wasn't gone, but he had found the secret: he wasn't meant to fight alone. He was meant to flow.

And in that flow, he was free.

13

Who Is Jesus?

The sanctuary was quiet after Wednesday night Bible study. Most people had already left, but Jamie lingered, staring at the open page before him. The passage was familiar, but tonight it felt alive:

"In the beginning was the Word, and the Word was with God, and the Word was God. The same was in the beginning with God. All things were made by Him; and without Him was not any thing made that was made. In Him was life; and the life was the light of men." (John 1:1–4)

Jamie read the verses again, his heart stirring. The Word. Logos. The divine expression. The conversation of God. The thoughts of God spoken into reality.

He whispered, "Jesus is the Word. The Logos. He is God's thought, God's heart, God's conversation made flesh."

Beyond Religion

As Jamie walked home, he reflected on what this meant. For years, he had thought of Jesus as a religious figure — Savior, yes, but somehow distant, locked in history, confined to Sunday sermons. But John 1 shattered that view.

Jesus wasn't an afterthought. He wasn't plan B. He was there in the beginning, the very expression of God. The divine conversation, present before creation, sustaining creation even now.

Jamie whispered into the night air, "You are not just part of my life. You are life."

The Word That Speaks

The next morning, Jamie sat at his kitchen table, journal open, Bible beside him. He thought about all the voices that filled his mind daily — fear, doubt, shame, ambition. And then he thought about Jesus, the Logos.

"If Jesus is the Word," he wrote, "then every time I hear Him, I am hearing God's thought. His divine expression. His eternal conversation. Every Scripture, every whisper in prayer, every nudge in my spirit — it's Him, speaking life."

For the first time, Jamie realized that listening to Jesus wasn't just devotional discipline. It was entering into the eternal conversation of God.

Plans of Hope

Later that week, Pastor Dan preached from Jeremiah 29:11–13:

"For I know the thoughts that I think toward you, saith the Lord, thoughts of peace, and not of evil, to give you an expected end. Then shall ye call upon Me, and ye shall go and pray unto Me, and I will hearken unto you. And ye shall seek Me, and find Me, when ye shall search for Me with all your heart."

Jamie felt the words pierce his soul. God's thoughts weren't random. They weren't harsh or condemning. They were thoughts of peace, hope, a future.

He scribbled furiously in his journal:

"Jesus is the Word — the Logos — the expression of God's thoughts. And Jeremiah says God's thoughts toward me are good, hopeful, filled with purpose. That means Jesus Himself embodies God's plan for me. He is my hope. He is my future."

Jamie leaned back, tears welling in his eyes. For the first time, he felt secure. His life wasn't drifting aimlessly. It was anchored in Jesus, the eternal Word, the One who carried God's hopeful thoughts over him.

A Conversation with Marcus

At lunch the next day, Marcus leaned across the table. "So, I've been meaning to ask. You talk about God a lot. But who's Jesus to you? I mean really?"

Jamie paused, surprised by the question. He set down his sandwich and thought carefully.

"Jesus... is everything. He's not just a teacher or a prophet. He's the Word — the Logos. The eternal expression of God. When I read Scripture, I'm not just reading text. I'm encountering Him. He's God's conversation with humanity. And He's God's plan for me. My hope. My future."

Marcus blinked. "So you're saying He's not just someone you believe in. He's someone you know."

Jamie nodded. "Exactly. He's the voice I hear when I'm lost. The light I see when it's dark. The hope I cling to when I don't know what's next. He's not just an idea. He's alive."

For once, Marcus didn't joke. He just sat back, quiet, as though the words had planted something deep inside.

Encounter in Prayer

That evening, Jamie went for a walk. The stars glimmered above, the night air cool on his skin. He found a quiet bench under a tree, sat down, and whispered, "Jesus, who are You, really?"

In the stillness, a verse surfaced in his heart: "In Him was life; and the life was the light of men."

Jamie closed his eyes, letting the words wash over him. He sensed it — the Logos, the Word, the divine conversation. Life itself, speaking directly to him.

For the first time, he didn't just believe Jesus was with him. He knew.

The Future Secure

Over the following days, Jamie's perspective shifted. When fear of the future rose, he remembered Jeremiah 29:11: "I know the thoughts I think toward you..." When loneliness pressed in, he remembered John 1: "In Him was life, and the life was the light of men."

One night, he journaled:

"Who is Jesus? He is the Word — Logos — God's conversation, God's thought, God's divine expression. He is life. He is light. He is the plan of God for my future, the hope that anchors me. He is not distant. He is here, now, speaking, breathing, living. And I will seek Him with all my heart."

Jamie closed the journal, peace washing over him. He finally understood. Jesus wasn't just the One who delivered, covered, or freed him. Jesus was the eternal Word — the very expression of God's heart.

And in knowing Him, Jamie had found everything he would ever need.

14

In Him Was Life

Jamie sat in his usual corner at the library, John 1:4 glowing from the page.

"In Him was life; and the life was the light of men."

He whispered it aloud, letting each word sink into his spirit. "In Him... was life. And that life was the light of men."

The word life stood out. He dug into his notes: Zoe — not just breathing, not mere existence, but the complete opposite of death. To be fully alive.

Jamie leaned back, heart pounding. So life isn't something I chase. Life is in Him. Real life. Zoe life. To be fully alive in Christ.

More Than Existing

Jamie thought about the past few years. He had survived, yes— gotten through workdays, paid bills, pushed through struggles. But had he really lived?

He shook his head. "Existing isn't the same as living." Zoe life was different. Zoe was abundant, overflowing, vibrant. It wasn't just waking up; it was being awake inside.

It wasn't just surviving storms; it was thriving in the presence of God, even in the storm.

Jamie whispered, "In You, Jesus, I don't just exist. I live."

The Light of Men

He turned to the next phrase: "And the life was the light of men."

Light — Phos. To shine. Luminous by rays. The glory of God in and on us.

Jamie stared out the window at the sunlight streaming in, golden rays scattering across the table. "That's it. Life in Christ produces light. Zoe creates phos. When I'm fully alive in Him, His light shines through me."

It struck him that he wasn't meant to generate light on his own. Light was the byproduct of His life in him.

A Conversation with Rachel

That evening, Jamie met Rachel at the café.

"Something's been hitting me today," he said. "John 1:4. In Him was life — Zoe life. Not just surviving, but really alive. And that life became light — the phos, the glory of God shining through us."

Rachel stirred her tea thoughtfully. "So the more alive you are in Him, the more His light shines through you?"

Jamie nodded. "Exactly. It's not about me trying to shine brighter. It's about receiving His life. The rays of light are just the evidence of being alive in Him."

Rachel smiled softly. "That means even in my darkest moments, His light can still shine, because His life is still in me."

Jamie leaned forward. "Yes. That's what changes everything. We don't shine because we're strong. We shine because we're alive in Him."

A Test of Life and Light

The revelation was tested sooner than Jamie expected. The next week, a co-worker spread a rumor about him, questioning his integrity. His chest tightened with anger. He wanted to lash out, to defend himself harshly.

But in that moment, he heard the whisper: "In Me is life. And that life is light."

Jamie took a deep breath. Instead of retaliating, he calmly addressed the situation with grace, clearing the misunderstanding without malice.

Later, Marcus pulled him aside. "Man, I don't know how you stayed so calm. I would've blown up."

Jamie smiled faintly. "It wasn't me. It was the life of Jesus in me. That's the only reason I could shine light instead of darkness."

For the first time, Jamie realized others were seeing the difference. The light wasn't hidden. It was shining.

The Glory in and On Us

One night, Jamie prayed under the stars. "Lord, You said life in You is light. That means Your glory is in me. But it's not just in me — it's on me, radiating out."

As he prayed, he sensed God's presence like warm rays on his skin, illuminating him inside and out. Tears streamed down his face. "I'm not walking in darkness anymore. I am alive. I am light."

Fully Alive

Days turned into weeks, and Jamie carried this truth with him. When stress came, he reminded himself: In Him is life. When fear pressed in, he whispered: That life is the light of men.

Slowly, his countenance changed. People noticed joy in his eyes, peace in his tone, resilience in his spirit.

Rachel told him one afternoon, "Jamie, you look... alive. Like really alive."

He grinned. "That's because I am. Zoe life. The complete opposite of death. I've found it in Him."

A Journal Entry

That night, Jamie opened his journal and wrote:

"In Him was life — Zoe — the fullness of being alive, the opposite of death. And that life became light — Phos — God's glory shining through me. Lord, I don't just want to exist. I want to live in Your life. Let my living be radiant with Your light. Let people see not me, but the rays of Your glory. In You, I am fully alive."

He closed the journal, peace flooding his soul. For the first time in a long time, Jamie didn't just feel like he was surviving. He felt alive. And in that life, light radiated — the glory of God shining not only in him but through him.

15

Full of Grace and Truth

Jamie leaned over his Bible, his eyes fixed on John 1:14:

"And the Word was made flesh, and dwelt among us, (and we beheld His glory, the glory as of the only begotten of the Father,) full of grace and truth."

The words struck him like thunder: Full of grace. Full of truth.

He whispered them aloud. "Grace... and truth."

Grace: More Than a Favor

Jamie pulled out his notes: Grace (Charis) — favor and divine influence.

He had always thought of grace as pardon — the undeserved kindness of God wiping away his sins. But this definition went deeper. Grace wasn't only a covering; it was an influence. Grace didn't just forgive him; it changed him.

"Divine influence," he whispered. "Grace shapes me. Grace empowers me. Grace doesn't just get me to heaven — it makes me alive here."

He thought back to moments of weakness when he had cried for strength and found unexpected courage rising within him. That was grace.

Truth: The Foundation

Next, Jamie studied truth: Aletheia — from the root Alpha. The beginning. The first. The origin.

Truth wasn't just facts. Truth was the eternal foundation of reality, springing from God Himself. Jesus wasn't simply telling the truth; He was Truth embodied, Truth incarnate, the Alpha from which all things flow.

Jamie wrote in his journal:

"Grace lifts me. Truth grounds me. Grace transforms me. Truth anchors me. Jesus is both. Full of both."

A Conversation with Rachel

That evening, Jamie shared his thoughts with Rachel over coffee.

"Do you realize how powerful it is that Jesus is full of both grace and truth?" he said, excitement in his voice. "Grace is God's favor and influence, and truth is God's eternal foundation. He doesn't tilt one way or the other. He embodies both."

Rachel tilted her head. "So grace without truth... would be just letting things slide? And truth without grace... would crush us?"

"Exactly!" Jamie said. "But Jesus carries both perfectly. Grace rescues me when I fail. Truth keeps me from drifting into lies. Together, they form the glory of God."

Rachel smiled slowly. "That's why I feel safe with Him. He doesn't excuse sin, but He also doesn't condemn me. He forgives me and then teaches me to walk differently."

Jamie nodded, his heart swelling. "Yes. That's what changes us."

The Glory Revealed

One Sunday morning, as Jamie sat in the pews, the choir began to sing about the glory of God. The sanctuary filled with voices, and

Jamie's spirit stirred. He thought of John's words: "We beheld His glory... full of grace and truth."

Suddenly, he felt it — not just an idea but a presence. Grace wrapping him in love. Truth steadying his soul. Together, they radiated glory.

Tears streamed down his cheeks. "Lord, this is Your glory. Not thunder or lightning. Not fire from heaven. Your glory is Your Son — grace and truth together."

Grace in His Weakness

That week, Jamie stumbled. Old fears returned, whispering that he wasn't enough. For a moment, shame weighed him down. But then he remembered: Grace — divine influence.

He knelt by his bed, whispering, "Jesus, I can't do this. Influence me. Shape me."

And slowly, strength rose in him again. The shame lifted, replaced by quiet confidence. Grace had not only forgiven him; it had strengthened him to stand.

Truth in His Wandering

Another day, Jamie faced confusion at work. A moral shortcut was offered — one that promised quick gain. He wrestled with the temptation, but then truth surged in his mind: Aletheia. Alpha. The first foundation.

He realized, "If I choose this lie, I'm stepping off the foundation. But if I stay in truth, I stand secure."

He chose truth, even though it cost him comfort. And peace flooded his heart.

Living in the Balance

Over the following weeks, Jamie learned to walk in the balance of grace and truth. Grace lifted him when he stumbled. Truth steadied him when he wavered. Grace reminded him of God's love. Truth reminded him of God's holiness.

Together, they revealed glory — the visible expression of the invisible God.

A Journal Entry

One night, Jamie wrote:

"John 1:14 says Jesus is full of grace and truth. Grace — favor and divine influence. Truth — the eternal Alpha, the foundation of reality. Lord, let me live in both. Not swayed by empty grace that excuses, not crushed by cold truth that condemns. But alive in the fullness of You — grace lifting me, truth grounding me. This is Your glory, and I behold it."

As he set down his pen, peace filled his soul. He felt anchored. He felt lifted. He felt covered by glory.

And for the first time, he realized: living in Jesus meant living in both grace and truth — and that was freedom.

16

The Conversation Made Flesh

Jamie sat in his living room with his Bible open, reading John 1:14 again:

"And the Word was made flesh, and dwelt among us..."

But this time, something new stirred. He remembered the teaching: the Word wasn't just sound, wasn't just ink on parchment. It was the divine conversation. God's eternal dialogue of thought and purpose. And that conversation had become flesh.

He leaned back, overwhelmed. "The Conversation became a person. Jesus is God's Word embodied, walking, breathing — the divine thought clothed in skin."

Why Flesh?

He asked himself the question written in his notes: Why?

The answer was profound: because the law of entry into this world is flesh. God had formed humanity from the dust of the earth. To live, breathe, and move in this world, one needed a body.

Jamie sat still, letting that truth settle. Jesus didn't bypass the law of humanity. He embraced it. To rescue mankind, He entered as mankind. To redeem flesh, He became flesh.

Jamie whispered, "You didn't just talk from heaven. You stepped into my world."

Relating to the World

Another question rose: Why?

The answer was simple yet staggering: so that Jesus could relate to this world, and in turn, so that Jamie could relate to Him.

If Jesus had only come as spirit, Jamie thought, he could never have understood Him. But because Jesus came in flesh — hungry, tired, tempted, yet without sin — Jamie could see Him, touch Him, know Him.

And more than that, Jesus showed how to live in this world while drawing everything needed from the Father.

Jamie wrote in his journal:

"The Conversation became flesh so I could understand it, see it, follow it. Jesus lived in the same dust-body as me, yet pulled everything He needed from God. That means I can too."

A Conversation with Rachel

Over dinner one evening, Jamie tried to explain.

"Think about it," he said. "The Word became flesh. God could have sent His plan through angels or visions, but instead He clothed His conversation in skin. Why? Because the only legal way to live on this earth is through a body. So He came like us."

Rachel looked amazed. "So Jesus had to eat, sleep, walk, and live like we do?"

"Yes," Jamie nodded. "And because of that, He knows what it's like to be tired, to be hungry, to be tempted. He understands. That's why I can trust Him — He lived this life fully, but perfectly."

Rachel smiled softly. "So the Word became flesh so the Word could touch us."

Jamie grinned. "Exactly. God's conversation stepped into our conversation."

Pulling from Heaven While on Earth

The more Jamie thought, the more practical it became. Jesus lived in flesh, yet everything He needed came from heaven. When food was scarce, He multiplied bread. When storms rose, He spoke peace. When death came, He commanded life.

Jamie realized: If the Word became flesh to model life, then I too can pull heaven into earth while in flesh.

He whispered, "Lord, show me how to live like that — fully human, yet fully dependent on You."

A Test of Flesh

The lesson was tested quickly. Jamie's car broke down on the way to work, and frustration surged. He felt the weight of being human — limited, tired, stuck.

But then he remembered: The Word became flesh. Jesus lived this life. He pulled from heaven what He needed. So can I.

Right there on the roadside, Jamie prayed, "Lord, I don't just need a fix for my car. I need Your peace. Help me live this moment like You would."

Almost immediately, a calm settled over him. Within minutes, a stranger pulled over, offering help and even recommending a mechanic who charged fairly.

Jamie smiled as he rode along. "The Conversation really does meet me in my flesh."

Dwelling Among Us

One night, Jamie reread John 1:14: "And dwelt among us."

The Word didn't just pass through. Jesus dwelt, lived, walked, shared meals, cried tears. He stayed.

Jamie thought, *That means He's still here, dwelling with me now. Not distant, but present in my daily grind, my daily joy, my daily pain.*

Tears filled his eyes. "Lord, thank You for not just speaking from afar. Thank You for dwelling with me — in the middle of this messy world."

The Conversation Continues

Later, Jamie journaled:

"The Conversation became flesh. Why? Because the law of entry here is flesh. Why? So He could relate to me, and so I could see how to live here while pulling everything I need from heaven. Jesus, You didn't just give me words; You became the Word. You didn't just speak life; You lived it.

That means I can too. Your Conversation still continues in me."

He closed the journal with a deep sigh of contentment.

For the first time, Jamie didn't just see Jesus as Savior. He saw Him as the living Conversation of God — not locked in ancient texts but alive in human skin, alive in his daily walk.

And with that revelation, Jamie felt more connected to Christ than ever before.

17

❧

Then God Breathed

Jamie sat in his room, weary from the week. Work deadlines had piled up, bills were due, and the weight of life pressed heavy. He felt like nothing more than flesh, tied down by the grind of this world.

But then he remembered the verse from Genesis:

"And the LORD God formed man of the dust of the ground, and breathed into his nostrils the breath of life; and man became a living soul." (Genesis 2:7)

He whispered to himself, "Then God breathed…"

Dust Without Breath

Jamie imagined Adam, freshly formed from the dust — complete in structure but lifeless, motionless, silent. All the potential of humanity lay there, but nothing moved until God leaned down and breathed.

He wrote in his journal:

"Dust without breath is just dust. Flesh without spirit is lifeless. But when God breathed, man became more than matter — he became a living soul."

Jamie realized he had been living like dust again — shaped but weary, alive but empty. What he needed wasn't more striving; it was fresh breath from God.

The Breath That Lifts Us Above the World

As he prayed, Jamie recalled the note from his teaching: *We became living souls when God breathed in us so we wouldn't be subject to this world.*

That struck him deeply. God's breath didn't just animate Adam; it elevated him. Breath distinguished man from beast, spirit from dust, eternity from temporality.

Jamie whispered, "Lord, Your breath means I'm not bound by this world's limits. I carry heaven's air inside me."

A Conversation with Rachel

At lunch with Rachel, Jamie tried to explain.

"Have you ever thought about why God breathed into Adam?" he asked.

Rachel thought for a moment. "Because that's how He gave him life?"

"Yes," Jamie nodded, "but more than that. God's breath made Adam more than dust. It made him a living soul, connected to heaven. That means we were never meant to be fully subject to this world. We carry His breath. That changes everything."

Rachel's eyes widened. "So when we feel trapped by life — by bills, stress, pain — we can remember that God's breath means we're not defined by it?"

"Exactly," Jamie said, his voice firm. "We live here, but we're not bound here. The breath of God inside us connects us to something higher."

Breath in the Valley

A week later, Jamie found himself in a personal valley. His mother called with news of a health scare, and fear gripped him. He sat in his car, trembling, unsure how to respond.

Then Ezekiel 37 came to mind — the valley of dry bones. God had asked, "Can these bones live?" Ezekiel had answered, "O Lord GOD, You know." And God's command was clear: "Prophesy to the breath... and they lived, and stood upon their feet, an exceeding great army."

Jamie whispered, "Breathe, Lord. Breathe into this situation. Breathe into my mom's body. Breathe into my fear."

Peace washed over him, steady and strong. Later, his mom called back with good news — the doctors had found the issue early, and it was treatable. Jamie wept, thanking God. "Your breath makes dead things live again."

Breath in Worship

The following Sunday, as the worship team sang, Jamie closed his eyes and inhaled deeply, as though taking in more than oxygen. He whispered, "Breathe on me, Lord."

In that moment, it was as if heaven's air filled his lungs. Joy rose, peace surrounded him, strength renewed him. For the first time in weeks, he felt alive — fully alive.

He realized worship wasn't just singing; it was *breathing* — receiving from God, returning it back as praise.

Not Subject to the World

In the days that followed, Jamie held onto one phrase: not subject to this world.

When his paycheck came short, he whispered, "I'm not subject to this world. God is my provider."

When fear of the future returned, he prayed, "I'm not subject to this world. God orders my steps."

When temptation pressed in, he declared, "I'm not subject to this world. God's Spirit empowers me."

Slowly, the truth reshaped him. He wasn't just surviving earth. He was breathing heaven.

A Journal Entry

One night, Jamie wrote:

"Then God breathed... and man became a living soul. Lord, I am dust without You. But Your breath makes me alive. Not just alive to eat, work, and sleep — alive to You, alive to eternity, alive beyond the limits of this world. Your breath sets me free from being subject to this world. Breathe on me again and again until every part of me lives in Your Spirit."

He closed the journal, a quiet smile on his face. He finally understood: he wasn't just dust. He was dust filled with divine breath.

And with that revelation, Jamie felt lighter, freer, as if the very air around him shimmered with heaven's presence.

18

Who Told You?

Jamie sat on his porch, the evening air still and heavy. His Bible lay open to Genesis 3:9–11. He read slowly:

"And the LORD God called unto Adam, and said unto him, Where art thou? And he said, I heard Thy voice in the garden, and I was afraid, because I was naked; and I hid myself. And He said, Who told thee that thou wast naked?"

Jamie whispered the last line again. "Who told you that you were naked?"

The question pierced him. God wasn't asking for information. God was exposing the source of Adam's new, broken conversation.

Jamie leaned back, trembling. "What conversation have I wrapped myself in?"

Voices That Shape

Memories flooded Jamie's mind — words spoken over him in childhood, cruel jokes in school, harsh criticism at work. He had wrapped himself in those conversations, carrying them like invisible clothing.

"You're not enough."

"You'll always fail."

"You'll never measure up."

They weren't God's words. But he had believed them. Just like Adam believed the serpent's whisper, Jamie had clothed himself in lies.

He whispered, "Lord... who told me? Who told me I was worthless? Who told me I was abandoned? It wasn't You."

The Wrong Conversation

That night, Jamie journaled:

"Adam wasn't naked for the first time that day. He had always been naked. But now, for the first time, he saw his nakedness through another voice — the serpent's. He wrapped himself in a false conversation of shame. Lord, how many times have I done the same? How many lies have I wrapped around myself?"

He closed the journal with tears streaming. He realized the real battle wasn't just around him — it was within him, in the conversations he allowed to define him.

A Conversation with Rachel

The next day, Jamie opened up to Rachel.

"Genesis 3 hit me hard," he admitted. "When God asked Adam, 'Who told you?', I felt like He was asking me. Who told me I was broken? Who told me I was unworthy? Those weren't God's conversations, but I've lived in them."

Rachel nodded slowly. "I think we all do. We wear voices like clothes. The problem is, most of those voices never came from God."

Jamie's voice broke. "Exactly. And I realized — I've been hiding from God, not because He shamed me, but because I believed someone else's words."

Rachel reached across the table and touched his hand. "Then maybe it's time to change the conversation."

Confronting the Lies

That evening, Jamie stood before the mirror in his room. He looked at his reflection, hearing the old words echoing in his head: Failure. Weak. Not enough.

But this time, he answered out loud.

"Who told me that? Not God."

"Who told me I was worthless? Not God."

"Who told me I was unloved? Not God."

Then he declared God's words instead:

"I am fearfully and wonderfully made."

"I am chosen, not forsaken."

"I am His workmanship, created for good works."

As he spoke, he felt the false conversations unravel, like old garments falling away. For the first time, he felt unclothed of shame — and clothed in truth.

Wrapped in the Right Conversation

Over the next few days, Jamie practiced a new discipline. Whenever a negative thought arose, he asked himself, "Who told me that?"

If it didn't match God's Word, he discarded it.

If it aligned with God's promises, he embraced it.

Slowly, he began to wrap himself in the right conversation — Scripture, prayer, encouragement.

At work, when Marcus mocked him, Jamie no longer shrank inside. He whispered under his breath, "Who told me I wasn't strong enough? Not God. He says His strength is made perfect in weakness."

The more he did it, the freer he felt.

The Garden Revisited

One night, Jamie dreamed he was walking through a garden. He heard footsteps and hid behind a tree, ashamed. But then a gentle voice called, "Jamie, where are you?"

He stepped out, trembling. "I heard Your voice... and I was afraid."

The voice spoke again: "Who told you that? Who told you fear was your covering? Who told you shame was your clothing? I never said that. I call you beloved. I call you mine."

Jamie woke with tears on his face. The dream felt more real than life. He whispered in the dark, "I hear You, Lord. I hear the right conversation now."

A Journal Entry

Later that week, Jamie wrote:

"What conversation have I wrapped myself into? Too often, it's been lies — shame, fear, doubt. But today, I choose to wrap myself in God's Word. I choose to clothe myself in His truth. Lord, let Your conversation be the only one that defines me. When You call, I will not hide. I will step into the light, wrapped in Your voice."

He set down the pen, feeling lighter than he had in years.

The Freedom of God's Voice

From that day, Jamie lived with a new question always on his lips: "Who told me?"

When doubt rose, he asked it.

When fear whispered, he asked it.

When shame knocked, he asked it.

And every time, the false conversation unraveled a little more.

In its place, God's true conversation wrapped around him — not garments of shame, but robes of righteousness, woven from grace and truth.

Jamie finally understood: what you believe shapes what you wear. And he chose to wear the conversation of God.

19

Another Conversation

Jamie sat at the park, Bible open on his lap, replaying Genesis in his mind. He whispered aloud:

"The devil presented Adam and Eve to another conversation... and at that point, they realized they were naked."

The phrase cut through him like a knife.

When Conversations Shift

Adam and Eve had walked in God's conversation daily — hearing His voice, knowing His presence. But one day, a new voice entered. The serpent's question was subtle:

"Did God really say...?"

Jamie shook his head. "That's all it took — another conversation."

He realized it wasn't just about fruit or trees. It was about attention. Whoever captured their conversation captured their reality.

He whispered, "The serpent's words didn't just tempt them — they reframed how they saw themselves. That's why they felt naked."

Nakedness as Exposure

Jamie thought about the word naked. Adam and Eve had always been without clothes, yet before, it was innocent. Covered by God's voice, they had no shame. But once another conversation entered, they saw themselves differently. What was once covered by glory now felt exposed.

Jamie wrote in his journal:

"Another conversation always strips me. It leaves me uncovered, ashamed, vulnerable. When I let fear speak louder than faith, I feel exposed. When I believe lies instead of truth, I feel unworthy. Another conversation always leads to nakedness."

Jamie's Own "Other Conversations"

He thought back to his own life — the moments he had stepped into conversations God never authored.

There was the time fear told him he wasn't safe. The time doubt told him he wasn't called. The time temptation told him compromise would feel good.

Each time, he left God's voice and listened elsewhere. And each time, he ended up ashamed, hiding, covered in fig leaves of excuses.

He whispered, "Lord, I've had my share of serpent-conversations. And every time, I've walked away feeling naked."

A Conversation with Rachel

Later, Jamie shared the revelation with Rachel.

"You know what hit me?" he said. "Adam and Eve weren't naked because their bodies changed. They were naked because the conversation changed. The serpent's words stripped them."

Rachel frowned thoughtfully. "So when I feel ashamed or inadequate, maybe it's because I've been listening to another conversation?"

"Exactly," Jamie said. "God's words cover us in glory. The enemy's words strip us with shame. The difference is whose voice we let define us."

Rachel's eyes filled with tears. "That explains so much. I've been listening to the wrong conversation about myself for years."

Jamie reached across the table. "Me too. But we don't have to stay there. We can choose the right voice."

Recognizing the Serpent's Voice

Over the next few days, Jamie paid close attention to his inner thoughts. Whenever shame, fear, or condemnation rose, he asked:

"Whose conversation is this?"

If it accused, shamed, or stripped him, he recognized it: serpent-talk. Another conversation.

And he began answering back:

"That's not what God said."

One morning, as doubt whispered, "You'll never overcome this," Jamie replied aloud, "God says I am more than a conqueror."

When fear said, "You're not safe," he declared, "God says no weapon formed against me shall prosper."

Slowly, he began to discern the difference between voices — and cling to the right one.

The Covering of the Right Conversation

Jamie realized something profound: God's conversation was not just information — it was covering.

When he listened to God's Word, he felt clothed in peace, wrapped in strength, shielded by truth.

When he drifted into another conversation, he felt stripped, exposed, vulnerable.

He whispered in prayer, "Lord, keep me wrapped in Your voice. Don't let me wander into serpent-talk again."

A Dream of Two Voices

One night, Jamie dreamed he was walking down a path. On one side, he heard a gentle voice speaking peace, promise, and life. On the other side, a hiss whispered doubt, shame, and fear.

He felt torn, caught between them. But then he saw himself — clothed in light as he leaned toward the voice of God, or stripped and shivering when he leaned toward the serpent.

He woke with a jolt, heart racing. The message was clear:

Whichever voice he chose to entertain would determine whether he felt clothed or naked.

A Journal Entry

The next morning, Jamie wrote:

"The devil presented Adam and Eve to another conversation, and they realized they were naked. Lord, I see now — conversations shape clothing. Your Word clothes me with righteousness, peace, and confidence. The enemy's words strip me with shame and fear. Help me discern every conversation and cling only to Yours. I don't want to be naked again. I want to stay covered in You."

He set down the pen, feeling renewed.

A New Resolve

From that day, Jamie made a choice: he would measure every thought, every whisper, every conversation by one standard:

Does this voice clothe me or strip me?

If it clothed him in peace, hope, and truth — it was God.

If it stripped him with shame, fear, and lies — it was the enemy.

And with that resolve, he began to walk in new confidence — clothed not in fig leaves of self-effort, but in the covering of God's voice.

2 0

Covered by Shame or Covered by Gl

Jamie sat quietly at his desk, pen hovering over his journal, reading the words again:

"Why was their first natural instinct to cover themselves? Because we were created to be covered. So you will either be covered by shame or covered by Glory."

He whispered aloud, "We were created to be covered."

It hit him harder than ever before.

The First Instinct

Adam and Eve's first reaction after sin was not to argue, deny, or blame — though blame came later. Their very first instinct was to grab leaves and cover themselves.

Jamie reflected, "They didn't even know what clothes were, yet something inside them screamed, 'I can't stay uncovered.'"

That natural instinct wasn't random. It revealed humanity's design: created to dwell under covering.

Jamie underlined in his Bible:

"And the eyes of them both were opened, and they knew that they were naked;

89

and they sewed fig leaves together, and made themselves aprons." (Genesis 3:7)

"Lord," Jamie prayed, "You designed us to be covered — not in leaves of shame but in Your glory."

Covered by Glory Before the Fall

Jamie imagined Adam and Eve before sin. Their bodies were bare, yet they weren't exposed. They were clothed in glory — radiant with God's presence, fully alive in His voice. That glory was their true garment.

He whispered, "So when sin entered, glory lifted... and they reached for fig leaves."

It dawned on him: **sin always substitutes glory with shame.**
And humanity is left desperately sewing coverings that never last.

Jamie's Own Fig Leaves

He thought of his own life. He hadn't reached for literal leaves, but he had sewn plenty of coverings.

When fear told him he wasn't enough, he hid behind achievements. When shame whispered about his past, he masked it with smiles. When doubt claimed he was unworthy, he drowned it in busyness.

Each of these were fig leaves — human attempts to cover what only God's glory could.

He wrote in his journal:

"Lord, every time I cover myself with performance, people-pleasing, or pride, I'm just sewing fig leaves. But You designed me for glory, not shame."

A Conversation with Pastor Lewis

One Sunday after service, Jamie shared his revelation with Pastor Lewis.

"Pastor, why do we always try to cover ourselves when we mess up?" Jamie asked.

Pastor Lewis smiled. "Because, son, you were created to be covered. It's not the instinct that's wrong — it's what you reach for. Adam reached for leaves. God offered skins of sacrifice. One covering was temporary. The other was a foreshadow of Christ."

Jamie leaned in. "So the question isn't whether I'll be covered — it's what will cover me?"

"Exactly," Pastor Lewis said. "Either shame will cover you... or glory will. And only Christ gives glory back."

Covered by Shame

Jamie thought about how shame works. Shame doesn't only remind us of what we've done — it becomes a garment.

Shame wraps itself around the heart, whispering:

You're unworthy.

You're dirty.

You'll never change.

Jamie remembered seasons where shame shaped everything he did — how he prayed, how he saw himself, how he related to people. Shame was a covering: heavy, suffocating, unrelenting.

But he compared it to the moments he had felt God's glory — worship, prayer, obedience — those moments where light wrapped him, peace covered him, and love embraced him.

One covering suffocated.

The other set him free.

An Encounter in Worship

At midweek service, Jamie lifted his hands as worship rose.

As the music swelled, the weight of shame — the mistakes, the regrets, the failures — began to peel off. Warmth and peace settled on him like a garment being placed deliberately over his shoulders.

He whispered, "Lord, cover me again. Not with leaves, but with Your glory."

Tears streamed down his face. In that moment, he knew he was clothed again — not by effort, but by presence.

A Dream of Two Robes

That night, Jamie dreamed he stood in a massive hall with two garments laid before him. One was torn, filthy, and unbearably heavy. The other glowed, soft and brilliant.

A voice asked, "Which covering will you wear?"

Jamie lifted the heavy garment first — shame — and as it touched him, he felt crushed, breathless, small.

Then he lifted the glowing robe. As soon as it brushed his shoulders, he felt weightless. Whole. Radiant.

The voice whispered, "This is glory. This is what I made you for."

He woke with tears on his pillow, whispering, "Lord, cover me with glory every day."

Journal Entry

The next morning, Jamie wrote:

"We are created to be covered. Instinct tells us to hide, but only glory can truly clothe us. Shame strips, glory restores. Every day, I choose: leaves or glory. Lord, wrap me in Your glory."

Living in Glory's Covering

Jamie started noticing something new: every action, thought, and reaction revealed which covering he was wearing.

When shame covered him, he withdrew, doubted, hid.

When glory covered him, he stepped boldly, loved freely, lived joyfully.

It wasn't about perfection — it was about choosing whose covering he lived under.

His new morning prayer became:

"Lord, today let me wear Your glory, not my shame."

A Closing Thought

Jamie realized this truth would stay with him forever:

"We are created to be covered. It's not a question of *if* we'll be covered, but *by what*.

Shame covers us when we listen to lies.

Glory covers us when we stay in God's voice.

Lord, let my instinct always draw me back to Your covering."

And with that truth, Jamie stepped into deeper freedom — clothed not in the weight of shame but in the radiance of God's glory.

21

Remain in the Glory

Jamie's journal was filling quickly these days. Each entry seemed to dig deeper, layer upon layer. He had just finished writing about coverings — shame versus glory — when another phrase struck him:

"To remain in the Glory we must cover or submit ourselves under the conversation or the Word God has about us."

Jamie underlined it three times: **Remain in the Glory.**

The Weight of the Word

As Jamie read the phrase again, one word leaped off the page: **Conversation.**

"Lord," he prayed quietly, "You've been teaching me that it's Your Word — Your divine Conversation over my life — that defines me. But remaining in it? That's the challenge."

He thought about his own tendencies — how quickly he shifted when trials came, how easily fear or doubt set the tone. Competing conversations constantly fought to define him.

One voice said, *You're not enough.*

Another whispered, *You'll fail just like before.*

But God's Word declared, *You are loved. You are chosen. You are Mine.*

The battle wasn't about which voice spoke — it was about which voice Jamie would remain under.

An Afternoon with Rachel

Later that week, Jamie visited his sister Rachel. Over coffee, she asked how his spiritual journey was going.

"Honestly," he admitted, "I've learned I live under competing conversations. God says one thing, but fear and shame say another. If I don't stay submitted under God's Word, I slip back under the weight of lies."

Rachel nodded. "It's like we choose which roof to stand under. One leaks shame. The other pours glory."

Jamie laughed. "Exactly. And the only way to stay in the glory is to keep myself under His Word — the Conversation."

Rachel grew thoughtful. "So the question isn't, *Will you be under a covering?* It's, *Which covering will you remain under?*"

Jamie smiled. "Yes. Remaining in the glory isn't a one-time choice. It's daily submission."

The Power of Remaining

That night, Jamie opened to John 15 again: *"Abide in Me, and I in you."*

He realized abiding wasn't passive — it was intentional. To remain in the glory, he had to continually align himself with God's conversation.

When fear spoke, he had to answer with Scripture.
When shame whispered, he had to remember he was covered by Christ's blood.
When doubt argued, he had to declare God's promises.

Remaining was resistance.
Remaining was warfare.

Remaining was worship.

A Wrestling Season

Over the next month, Jamie faced one of his hardest seasons. Work pressures intensified. His mother's health declined. Discouragement began to creep in.

One night, alone in his apartment, he felt old temptations and lies rise like shadows.

"Why keep trying?" a voice hissed. "You'll never change. Just give up."

Jamie almost yielded. But suddenly something in him cried out:

"The Conversation! The Conversation!!!"

He grabbed his Bible and read aloud:

"No weapon formed against you shall prosper."

"Greater is He that is in you than he that is in the world."

"I know the plans I have for you... plans to give you a future and a hope."

As he spoke, the atmosphere shifted. The lies lost their power.

"Lord," Jamie whispered, "I choose to remain in Your conversation."

A Vision in Prayer

A few nights later, Jamie dreamed he was standing in a massive hall filled with voices. Some shouted accusations, some whispered shame, some mocked him.

In the center was a beam of light, and in that light, a single voice spoke Scripture — identity, hope, truth, life.

Jamie realized the voices would never stop. But he could choose where to stand.

With determination, he stepped into the beam of light. Instantly, the other voices faded. Glory surrounded him. Peace filled him.

The voice said, "Remain here. Remain in My Word. Remain in My glory."

He woke with tears on his face, whispering, "The Conversation... The Conversation... The Conversation."

Daily Practice

Jamie began a new habit: every morning, he declared three Scriptures over his life. He called it **"staying under the Conversation."**

At work, he whispered them during stress.

At night, he repeated them when fear tried to creep in.

Slowly, remaining became not just something he practiced — but something he lived.

A Conversation with Pastor Lewis

One Sunday, Jamie shared his discovery with Pastor Lewis.

"Pastor," Jamie said, "I've realized remaining in the glory isn't about feelings. It's about submission — choosing to stay under what God says, no matter what I feel or face."

Pastor Lewis grinned. "Jamie, you've learned the secret. The enemy will always offer alternative conversations. But glory remains where God's Word is honored. Stay under the Conversation, and you'll stay in the glory."

Jamie nodded. "The Conversation. Always the Conversation."

A Closing Thought

Jamie ended his journal entry with a powerful truth:

"Remaining in glory is remaining in God's Word. To remain, I must continually cover myself in the Conversation He speaks. Other voices shout, but His Word wraps me in light. Lord, let me never step out from under Your covering."

A deep strength rose inside him — not a fleeting emotion, but a steady foundation.

He whispered aloud, almost like worship:

"The Conversation... The Conversation... The Conversation."

22

The Conversation Disrupter

Jamie sat in his living room late at night, Bible open, when his eyes fell on the book of Job. The words unsettled him:

"Now there was a day when the sons of God came to present themselves before the Lord, and Satan came also among them. And the Lord said unto Satan, Whence comest thou?
Then Satan answered the Lord, and said, From going to and fro in the earth, and from walking up and down in it." (Job 1:6–7)

Jamie leaned back in his chair, heart heavy. *Even in Job's time, the enemy was already showing up to interfere with the conversation about someone's life.*

It wasn't new.

It wasn't random.

It was strategy.

The Enemy's Tactic: Disruption

Jamie thought back over his own journey. How many times had he felt on fire after a revelation — only to find himself discouraged the very next day?

After learning to abide, fear came knocking.

After walking in freedom, shame whispered again.

99

After deciding to remain in glory, distractions screamed louder.

It dawned on him: **the enemy always comes to disrupt the conversation.**

Satan didn't begin Job's trial by attacking his body or wealth. He started by **challenging the conversation** God declared about Job's character.

Jamie whispered, "The attack isn't always on what I have. It's on the conversation over my life."

A Test at Work

The following week, Jamie faced a real-life example. His manager had praised his work ethic and hinted at a promotion. But a jealous co-worker began spreading rumors:

"Jamie only gets noticed because he pretends to be so spiritual. It's fake."

When Jamie overheard it, his stomach dropped. Anger rose — but beneath it was a familiar, painful whisper:

See? You're not really who you think you are. It's all an act.

For a moment, he almost believed it. But then he remembered the scene from Job.

"This isn't about rumors," he whispered. "This is about the conversation."

The enemy was attempting to disrupt what God had spoken:
You are chosen. You are mine. You are faithful in little, so I can trust you with more.

Jamie closed his eyes. "Lord, I refuse to let lies rewrite Your conversation over my life."

Jesus the Redirector

That Sunday, Pastor Lewis preached from Jesus' baptism:
"This is My beloved Son, in whom I am well pleased."

Pastor's voice rang out across the sanctuary:

"Before Jesus worked one miracle, preached one sermon, or healed one person — the Father established the conversation: **Beloved. Pleasing. Approved.**

And immediately after that, the Spirit led Him into the wilderness — where Satan tried to disrupt it."

Jamie felt chills. Every temptation began with, *"If you are the Son of God..."*

Satan wasn't just trying to make Jesus sin; he was trying to **break the conversation** spoken by the Father.

But Jesus answered every disruption the same way:

"It is written..."

Jamie scribbled in his journal:

The enemy disrupts.

Jesus redirects.

He always takes me back to what God has spoken.

Every temptation is a test of conversation.

Every victory is a return to truth.

The Whisper of the Spirit

In the days that followed, Jamie noticed something new. Whenever discouragement whispered, another voice gently rose inside him:

"You are loved."

"You are chosen."

"You are forgiven."

"You are free."

At first, Jamie thought it was just memory reciting Scripture. But during prayer one night, Pastor Lewis clarified:

"The Spirit's ministry is to remind you of the conversation. He is the echo of Heaven inside you, pointing you back to what the Father has already said."

Jamie broke down in tears. "So I'm never alone in this battle. Even when the enemy disrupts, the Spirit reminds."

A Vision of the Courtroom

One night Jamie dreamed of a courtroom. Satan stood as an accuser, shouting:

"He's unworthy! He's weak! He will fail again!"

Jamie felt small, overwhelmed — until Jesus stepped forward as his advocate.

Calmly, with authority, Jesus declared:

"This one belongs to Me. The Father has already spoken:

Beloved. Redeemed. Free.

This is the conversation."

The Judge struck the gavel.

"Case dismissed."

Jamie woke up with a peace he couldn't explain.

Journal Entry

The next morning he wrote:

*"The devil disrupts.

Jesus redirects.

The Spirit reminds.

Lord, help me never confuse the noise of accusation with the truth of the conversation.

My life is not defined by disruption but by divine declaration."*

Living the Reality

From then on, Jamie built a habit: whenever accusations rose — through people, thoughts, or fear — he paused and asked:

"Whose conversation am I listening to right now?"

If it was disruption, he answered with Scripture.

If it was silence, he waited for the Spirit's whisper.

If it was glory, he stayed under it.

Attacks still came.

Accusations still surfaced.

But they no longer rewrote his identity.

Jamie learned to stand firm — not by fighting harder, but by returning to the Conversation God had already spoken.

A Closing Thought

Jamie realized the real war wasn't over his possessions, reputation, or even future.

It was over the conversation about his life.

He said aloud:

"The devil disrupts — but Jesus redirects me back to truth. And the Spirit always reminds me.

Lord, keep me tuned to Heaven's conversation."

And with that, Jamie felt equipped — not just to survive disruption, but to live anchored in the ongoing Conversation of God's glory.

23

Present Yourself

Jamie sat with his Bible open to Romans 10, whispering the words slowly:

"But what does it say? The word is near you, in your mouth and in your heart (that is, the word of faith which we preach): that if you confess with your mouth the Lord Jesus and believe in your heart that God has raised Him from the dead, you will be saved.

For with the heart one believes unto righteousness, and with the mouth confession is made unto salvation.

For the Scripture says, 'Whoever believes on Him will not be put to shame.'"

He read it again. And again.

"This is it," he thought. **"This is what it means to present myself."**

The Meaning of "Present"

In his notes, Jamie circled the word *present* and wrote the Hebrew root: **yatsab**.

To be placed under.

To offer.

To stand in.

It wasn't just showing up. It was **surrendering**.
It was stepping willingly under the covering of God's conversation, placing himself fully within its truth.

Jamie whispered, "To present myself means to stand under what You say, Lord — not my feelings, not my fears, not the enemy's lies. Only the Conversation."

A Practical Test

That week, Jamie had a chance to put it into practice.

He was scheduled to give a work presentation. As he prepared, anxiety gnawed at him:

What if you stumble?
What if they think you're not good enough?

He almost backed out. But then Romans 10 rose in his heart again: *The word is near you, in your mouth and in your heart.*

Jamie paused. "Lord, today I present myself. Not under fear. Not under insecurity. But under the Word You've spoken about me."

As he walked into the meeting room, he whispered, **"Yatsab — I stand in the Conversation."**

The presentation flowed smoothly. His colleagues applauded. But more than their approval, Jamie felt peace. He had chosen his covering — and it was the Word.

A Conversation with Pastor Lewis

After Sunday service, Jamie approached Pastor Lewis.

"Pastor, I realized presenting myself isn't about showing up to church. It's about choosing daily to stand under God's Word. Even at work, I had to consciously put myself under His conversation instead of fear."

Pastor Lewis smiled. "Jamie, that's the essence of surrender. We often present ourselves under false conversations: fear, pride, doubt. But

Scripture calls us to offer ourselves as living sacrifices. That posture isn't passive — it's deliberate."

"So every time I choose to stand in His Word," Jamie asked, "I'm presenting myself?"

"Exactly," Pastor replied. "Romans 10 reminds us: when you believe in your heart and confess with your mouth, you're aligning your whole being — heart and lips — under His conversation. That is true presentation."

A Mirror Moment

Later that week, Jamie stood in front of his bathroom mirror. His reflection showed tired eyes and a faint shadow of worry.

For years, mirrors reminded him of his flaws. But tonight he whispered Romans 10:11:
"Whoever believes on Him will not be put to shame."
Slowly, Jamie declared:

"I present myself under that Word. I am not defined by shame. I am defined by His conversation."

Something shifted. For the first time in years, Jamie didn't just see his face — he saw a man covered by glory.

A Dream of Surrender

One night, Jamie dreamed he was standing in a vast open field. Before him were two banners:

One was marked by accusation: *Failure. Weak. Not Enough.*
The other radiated with life: *Chosen. Loved. Redeemed.*

A voice asked, "Where will you stand?"

Jamie hesitated. The banner of accusation felt familiar — almost comfortable.

But then he remembered: **yatsab — to stand in, to offer myself under.**

With a deep breath, he walked under the banner of life. Light wrapped around him instantly. Peace filled his heart.

He woke with clarity: "Every day, I choose where to present myself."

Journal Entry

Jamie wrote:

"Presenting myself is surrender. It is choosing to place my whole being under the conversation God speaks.

Every fear demands I present myself under it.

Every lie offers a false covering.

But the Spirit calls me daily: Stand in My Word. Offer yourself here. Present yourself under the Conversation."

A Closing Revelation

Jamie realized presenting himself wasn't a single altar moment — it was a **daily posture**.

Every morning.

Every decision.

Every temptation.

He had to ask:

Where will I stand?

What conversation will I offer myself to?

As he closed his journal, he whispered:

"Lord, today, I present myself under Your Word.

The Conversation! The Conversation! The Conversation!"

And with that prayer, Jamie stepped into a new rhythm — living not under fear or shame, but under the divine covering of God's eternal Conversation.

24

The Conversation is Close

Jamie stood on the balcony of his apartment as the sun rose over the horizon. The morning air was crisp, carrying the fragrance of dew. Birds sang in the trees, their voices harmonizing with the silence of dawn.

He breathed deeply, whispering, "The Conversation is close... in my mouth and in my heart."

For years, he had struggled to believe that God's Word was really that near. He had fought shame, wrestled with doubt, battled through lies, and stumbled under the weight of fear. But now — after walking this long road — he knew: the Word was not far off. It wasn't unreachable. It wasn't locked away in Heaven or buried deep in mystery.

It was here. Inside him. Alive and powerful.

Jamie smiled, a quiet fire burning in his eyes. "Lord, I know who I am. I know whose I am. And I will never again live beneath the Conversation You have spoken over me."

The Power of the Spoken Word

That morning, Jamie prepared to meet his coworkers for a volunteer project. They were helping rebuild a community center in one of the rougher neighborhoods nearby. As he got ready, he repeated Scriptures aloud, almost like a song:

"I am more than a conqueror through Christ who loves me."
"Greater is He that is in me than he that is in the world."
"The Word is near me, in my mouth and in my heart."

With every declaration, his spirit grew stronger. He realized that victory wasn't silent — **it was spoken**. When he opened his mouth in faith, Heaven's Conversation became audible on earth.

By the time he arrived at the project site, Jamie wasn't just ready to build walls and paint rooms. He was ready to speak life into everyone he met.

A Witness at Work

As Jamie carried supplies into the center, Marcus pulled him aside. Usually sarcastic and skeptical about faith, Marcus looked unusually serious.

"Jamie," he said quietly, "I don't get it. You've been through a lot — stress at work, your mom's health... all of it. But you don't break like the rest of us. You've got this... peace. What's your secret?"

Jamie's heart swelled. This was the moment.

"It's not me," he said. "It's the Word. God's Conversation about me is stronger than anything life throws my way. And it's not just for me — it's for you too."

Marcus frowned. "The Word? Conversation? What are you talking about?"

Jamie opened his small Bible and read from Romans 10:

"The word is near you, in your mouth and in your heart — that is, the word of faith we preach."

He looked Marcus in the eyes. "God's not far off. His Word isn't distant. It's right here, waiting for you to believe it and speak it. That's the secret. That's the power."

Marcus didn't reply, but something in him softened.

Drawing Others to Faith

Later that afternoon, during lunch, Jamie's friend Alyssa approached him hesitantly.

"I overheard what you told Marcus," she said. "Everything feels so empty lately. Do you really believe God has a Word for me too?"

Jamie nodded. "Absolutely. The Conversation isn't just about me. It's about anyone who will receive it. Jesus came for the searching, the broken, the tired. And Alyssa — that includes you."

Tears welled in her eyes. "I want that. I want His Conversation to cover me too."

Right then, on the steps of the community center, Jamie prayed with her. She confessed Jesus as Lord and believed that God raised Him from the dead. As she prayed, peace washed over her. She laughed softly through tears.

"I feel... lighter. Like something broke off me."

Marcus, still listening, muttered, "Maybe there's something real here after all."

Jamie grinned. "There is. And Marcus, whenever you're ready, the Conversation is waiting for you too."

The Ripple Effect

Word spread among Jamie's friends and coworkers. Some came curious. Others came hungry. They saw a man who once wore shame now walking boldly in glory. They saw consistency — not perfection — but steady transformation through the Word.

At work, people who once mocked now asked for prayer.
In his family, Rachel and their mother found new strength through his encouragement.
At church, Pastor Lewis often pointed to Jamie as a living testimony of what happens when someone **remains under the Conversation**.

Jamie remembered Romans 10:17: *"Faith comes by hearing, and hearing by the Word of God."*

His voice, once silenced by shame, had become a vessel of faith for others.

A Dream of Victory

One night, Jamie dreamed he stood on a mountain overlooking the earth. Each time he declared God's Word, beams of light rose from his mouth, spreading across the horizon. Those waves of light touched the hearts of friends, coworkers, and even strangers.

Then the voice of the Lord spoke:

"This is the power of the Conversation. It is near you, in your mouth and in your heart. And through your witness, it will cover the earth."

Jamie woke in tears. "Lord, use me. Let my life be an echo of Your Conversation until the world knows You."

From Dust to Glory

As he reflected later, one final truth struck him: though he was formed from the dust of the ground, that dust was formed by God.

"If God can form dust," Jamie whispered, "He can form me into a vessel of glory."

He lifted his hands in worship. "Lord, You made me from dust, but You filled me with Your breath. Now let every breath I take proclaim Your Conversation."

The Grand Finale

Weeks later, Jamie stood in front of a packed room at the newly re-stored community center. To his surprise, the director invited him to speak.

He stepped up to the microphone, heart pounding with holy fire.

"My friends," he began, "we came to build walls and paint rooms. But God has been building something far greater in us. He's been reminding me that His Word is not far away. It's close. It's in your mouth and in your heart. And when you believe it and speak it, everything changes."

He scanned the crowd — Marcus in the back, Alyssa in the front, his mother and Rachel smiling proudly.

"The same Word that saved me, freed me, and covered me in glory is here for you. You don't have to live under shame. You don't have to live under lies. The Conversation is near — right here, right now."

Hands rose. Tears flowed. Voices whispered prayers.

Jamie saw it — a harvest of souls drawn not by his strength, but by the power of the Conversation flowing through him.

"Jesus Christ is Lord," he declared. "His Conversation is the final word. And through Him, we are more than conquerors!"

The room erupted in applause — but Jamie knew the real celebration was happening in Heaven.

A Closing Picture

That night, Jamie returned to his balcony. He looked up at the stars and whispered:

"The Conversation is close. In my mouth. In my heart. In my life. Forever."

And as the night settled around him, Jamie knew he was no longer the man who doubted, feared, or hid in shame.

He was a man fully alive. Fully free. Fully covered in glory.

A living Conversation of faith — echoing into eternity.

Dr. Tony Medley Sr. is a pastor, teacher, mentor, and author whose life and ministry have been dedicated to helping people discover the power of God's Word spoken over their lives. Known for his passionate preaching and practical teaching, Dr. Medley has spent decades equipping believers to hear God's voice, walk in their identity in Christ, and live with purpose and bold faith. His ministry extends beyond the pulpit through books, training materials, stage plays, and discipleship resources designed to ignite transformation in individuals, churches, and communities. Dr. Medley combines deep biblical insight with everyday application, ensuring that readers not only understand the Scriptures but also live them out with confidence. With a message that is both prophetic and practical, Dr. Medley inspires people to see themselves through heaven's perspective. He believes every person is "wrapped in the conversation" of God and destined to thrive in His promises. When he is not writing or teaching, Dr. Medley is serving his church family, mentoring emerging leaders, and enjoying time with his own family, who remain his greatest earthly joy.